her Errant Earl

SCARLETT SCOTT

Her Errant Earl
Wicked Husbands Book One

dedication

For my dear Aunt Julia, who taught me how to sip tea
from a cinnamon stick, and who never allows me to forget
about the time we hid Gregory's pumpkins or the measure
of a good time.

contents

London, 1853

WILL WATCHED HIS MOTHER SURVEY the efforts of her lady's maid upon her hair, turning her head this way and that, admiring her own reflection. The duchess reminded him of the butterflies in the gardens of Carrington House. Bright and beautiful, forever flitting from one flower to the next. He longed for her presence, but she was always leaving.

"This will do, Ganley," she told the servant. "Thank heavens the third attempt took. Pray take more care studying the latest styles. I cannot spend so many hours each evening upon my *toilette*. You are dismissed."

The servant, who was always ready to sneak him sweets whenever he ventured belowstairs against the strict edict of his father the duke, curtseyed formally. Her expression was grave. His mother's rebuke had stung. "Thank you, Your Grace. I will again study the lady's magazines Your Grace has so kindly lent me this evening."

"Mind that you don't crease the pages, Ganley. I can't bear to look at a magazine that looks as if it's been riffled

1

through." The duchess directed a regal nod in Ganley's direction.

The lady's maid whisked her skirts past Will, but she took care to meet his gaze and give him a wink that told him she'd have his sweet ready when next they crossed paths. He certainly hoped it would be one of Mrs. Rufton's seed cakes. Perhaps even a curd tart. His stomach rumbled with anticipation at the thought. His father forbid him from eating sweets, saying they rotted the mind and body. All he was served in the nursery was cold meats and hard bread, the disciplined diet befitting a future duke, according to his father.

Will hated bread, and he hated cold meat, but he hated his father the most.

"William, darling," his mother trilled. "Come and give me a kiss before I must leave."

Another ball, he supposed. Or dinner. Or musical evening. Or the opera. She was eternally headed somewhere, and she was ever saying goodbye, calling for him just before her departure, all gilded and glittering and beautiful. He knew how to tell time. He had his own pocket watch, engraved with a Latin verse he'd yet to decipher. According to the timepiece, he spent less than ten minutes with his mother each day.

He didn't hate his mother. She wasn't cruel and harsh. She had never told him he was stupid or sinful or unworthy of being the heir to a duchy. She wasn't repressive or commanding. She didn't force him to eat cold meat and sleep with only one blanket and recite the bible with a tutor who caned him when he confused a verse. But neither did she stop his father from doing all of those things. Nor did she notice Will, aside from her daily call to join her as she completed her *toilette*, just so that she could disappear again, having committed her maternal obligation.

No, he didn't hate her, but he wished most wholeheartedly for her to *care*. For her to notice that he was her son and not another servant to dismiss at will so she could carry on with the next round of parties.

Dutifully, he crossed the soft carpets to her side, entering her enchanted circle just for a moment. She leaned down to buss a kiss on his cheek. Her perfume enveloped him so forcefully that he sneezed.

She drew back, a look of horror marring her features as she inspected her bodice. "William, just look at what you've done." Her tone was appalled.

Specks of his saliva mottled the otherwise flawless silk and lace of her pink gown. "Pray forgive me, Mother," he apologized.

"Now I shall have to call Ganley back, and I shall be late to the Featherston ball, you awful, careless boy." Her voice was shrill in her anger.

He winced. "I'm sorry for my imprudence."

"Sorry does not fix my gown. Do you understand?" She grabbed his shoulders with both hands, shaking him. "Have a care. You've ruined everything. You always ruin everything!"

"I'm so sorry," he said again, his teeth snapping together under the force of her violence. He thought then of what he'd meant to tell her, what he'd been planning all day. "Please, Mother. I found a puppy, and I mean to keep him but Father won't allow it. Can you tell Father to let me keep the puppy? I've named him Ferdinand."

She released him, making a sound of disgust. "You've ruined my dress, and all you can think of is yourself. Be gone from my sight. I've no more patience for you this evening."

"But Mother—"

"Be gone!" she yelled, her eyes dark with fury. "Gone, I say!"

Will bowed and left the chamber. He knew better than to remain when his mother was in one of her black moods. Off to the nursery he went with Miss Greenley. He washed his face and behind his ears and said his prayers before settling into bed for an uneasy sleep. When he woke the next morning, the puppy lay dead at the foot of his bed.

chapter one

VICTORIA AWOKE TO THE UNMISTAKABLE THUMPS of footsteps approaching her bed. It was devilishly dark in her chamber and she couldn't see a blessed thing. Her heart kicked into a frantic pace, threatening to gallop from her chest. As horror churned through her, she reached for the nearest weapon at hand, which turned out to be the novel she'd been reading earlier. Fortunately, it had just enough heft to do damage. Blessedly verbose fellow, that Dickens. As the unseen assailant approached her bed, she struck out in his general direction.

Thwack. She landed an appreciable blow in what she hoped was the scoundrel's face. How dare someone have the impudence to accost her, the Countess of Pembroke, in her bed? Had the world gone completely to the dogs?

"Blast it, woman," came a masculine growl through the murk. "I think you've broken my bloody nose."

Dear God, she knew that growl, knew it better than her own voice. It mattered little that she hadn't heard it in months. The velvety timbre hadn't changed one whit. Nor had its unwanted effect upon her.

4

"Pembroke?" she asked though she needn't have. "Is that you?"

"Yours as ever, madam." The voice was now muffled though redolent with derision. "Although that was not precisely the welcoming I expected."

"*You* weren't expected," she pointed out, making a concerted effort to squelch the sudden rush of jumbled emotion his appearance had stirred. She could not allow him to see how very much he distressed her.

"Nonsense. I live here."

"Indeed." She crossed her arms and glared at him, summoning the hurt and anger he'd dealt her. In the moonlight, she could discern only his broad silhouette, and how she wished she could see more. "Is it possible you've been hiding about in the kitchens with Mrs. Rufton for the last few months?"

"When did you acquire such a sharp tongue, my dear?"

He sounded surprised by her ire, the rogue. She hoped she had broken his nose. It would be a suitable punishment, a well-deserved imperfection to disrupt the masculine beauty of his face.

"One can take up any number of pursuits whilst abandoned in the country." She sighed. "Can you not at least light one of the lamps? I dislike being at a disadvantage to my enemy."

"Harsh words for your husband. Not even a kind remark or a kiss from your lovely lips?" There was a scuffling sound as she presumed he attempted to light the gas lamps.

That he would jest in such a moment of tumult infuriated her. Had he no feeling? No compunction? No inkling of how he'd torn her down as if she were no better than a crumbling garden wall, leaving her to grow lichens and moss on his vast estate? Being ignored was the gravest form of insult, for it showed an incredible dearth of compassion and feeling both. She must have meant less than nothing to him.

"You're more likely to receive a kiss from Mrs. Morton,"

she snapped.

"Who the devil is Mrs. Morton?" Light flared to life, making her absentee husband visible.

He was handsome as ever, the rotten cad, with thick mahogany hair worn a bit too long, blue eyes, a hint of whiskers shading his strong jaw, and high cheek bones. Some of the ice inside her melted, despite her firm determination to remain impervious. He'd had the same effect upon her from the moment she'd first seen him, and it was equal parts dizzying and infuriating. It wasn't merely that he was fine-looking and charming. There was some indefinable quality that drew women to him, some rare magnetism that made everyone in a room aware of him the instant he'd entered it, and it vexed her to admit she had fallen prey to his charisma herself.

But not any longer. He still stole her breath, much as he'd stolen her foolish heart. And she still resented him for both. It would seem that little had changed save the level of her exasperation.

"Mrs. Morton is the housekeeper," she explained to him through gritted teeth. She took great care to draw the counterpane up to her chin, all the better to defend herself.

"What became of Mrs. Grimshaw?" He looked truly perplexed. "Am I not to be made aware of changes in my own household? Why the devil didn't the steward tell me?"

"There is no steward at Carrington House. As you should know, there hasn't been one for some time. I wrote you a letter explaining Mrs. Grimshaw had unexpectedly passed on to her rewards and that we were in need of a replacement." She couldn't keep the scorn from her voice. She had been installed in his home for mere months and she already knew more of it than he, who had roamed its echoing halls and sprawling fields his entire life. But that was what Pembroke did, she'd discovered. He slipped through life, charming women, using his devastating good looks to his advantage, and happily ignoring all responsibilities. "Very likely you never deigned to read it."

"No steward? Bloody hell." He had the decency to look rather shamefaced at the revelation. "I'm afraid my secretary handles the bulk of my correspondence. I shall take him to task for not keeping me aware of the comings and goings of the estate."

"Yes," she agreed with feigned sweetness, "you certainly should. I'm quite sure it isn't as if you merely toss my epistles into the dustbin the instant you recognize my penmanship."

"I've never thrown away a single one of your letters." Pembroke frowned at her, revealing small furrows next to his eyes. Surely their original source was laughter, she thought, rather than displeasure. A man of his nature spent his days in nothing but self-indulgence and sin.

"Nor have you answered any of them." Not a single, blessed one. And she had sent many, varying in tone from polite to thoroughly aggrieved. Finally, she had simply stopped writing altogether, recognizing an exercise in futility when she saw one. "Indeed, I daresay you've never read them either."

If bitterness laced her words, there was ample reason for it. She'd been taught well by her mother how to treat her husband. He was to be honored and respected above all. Her proud parents, *nouveau riche* and not old blood enough for Knickerbocker elite in New York, had gone to great pains to secure an English title for her with their wealth. And secure one they had, such a feather in her cap. The heir to the Duke of Cranley, the very picture of fine, English masculinity. Her mother had returned to New York victorious, determined to follow the same course with her younger daughters.

Victoria had been left alone, mired in the misery of the unwanted. She was no longer an innocent miss who believed her husband cared whether or not she even breathed. He'd dazzled her in the ballroom and then promptly forgotten her on the first day of their honeymoon as he rode back to London and a score of scandalous women.

He sat on the edge of the bed and her gaze slipped to his hands. She recalled too well how they had felt on her body. But those hands had betrayed her, bringing the same forbidden pleasure to countless others in her stead. He caressed the line of her leg beneath the counterpane and she scooted away from his touch.

"I've missed you."

The pronouncement startled a laugh from her. She didn't trust him. Not one jot. "You've arrived in the midst of the night to tell me you missed me? Surely you can think of something more worthy of your silver tongue than that, Pembroke."

He shrugged as if he hadn't a care. Perhaps he didn't. After all, his life was nothing but one long string of balls, opera singers, and whisky-soaked nights. If only she'd realized the sort of man he truly was before becoming his wife, she would have spared herself a great deal of heartache and loneliness. She'd been left an ocean away from her parents and younger sisters, saddled with the duty of a grand and neglected manor and the knowledge that her husband was off reveling in his degenerate life of London decadence.

"I wasn't aware there were rules for arriving at my own residence." His hand found her leg again and slid higher, only the barriers of bedclothes and fabric between them. That voice of his was smooth and sinful and deep, putting her in mind of Odysseus and his Sirens. "I know I've been remiss."

His touch wasn't lost on her. He reached her inner thigh. It would be so easy to give in, allow him to nudge her legs apart, strip away the bedclothes... She had been able to accomplish a great many things during her time at Carrington House, yet she had not been able to become entirely resistant to her husband's lure. Even now, after months of silence as he betrayed her with half the ladies of London, his caress forced an unwanted trickle of need through her.

Still, that didn't mean she couldn't fight him.

She slapped at his hand as though he were an offending insect. "You may continue being remiss. I have no wish for your company now or ever."

He gave her a lazy smile, dimples bracketing his sculpted mouth. "I'm afraid you're about to suffer a great deal of my company."

Pembroke was one of the most handsome men she had ever seen on either side of the Atlantic, and the very worst part of this plain truth was that he knew it. He had a knack for flirting, for giving stolen kisses in the shadows of a ball. He had a gift for making women love him. He'd made *her* love him, once, though she'd done her best to bury all traces of that unwelcome emotion in the wake of his desertion. It was still difficult to resist his charm when he deigned to ply it, even if he collected hearts the way some men amassed tomes in a library.

"You'll be back in London in less than a fortnight," she predicted.

"I shall prove you wrong." He startled her by moving his caress to her cheek. He had never, not even during their courtship, touched her face. Just a slow, deliberate swipe of his thumb over her cheekbone, his long fingers cradling her jaw. Hardly anything, really. Hardly noteworthy, and yet it chipped at the careful boundary she'd crafted between them.

She tilted her head, severing the contact. "What do you want?"

But his hand merely continued its gentle travels elsewhere. Down the curve of her throat, then sliding to cup the base of her skull. His eyes scoured her face intently, as though she were a book whose meaning somehow evaded him. "Your hair is very pretty. Have I ever told you that?"

"No." She eyed him warily. There was a time when she would have welcomed his praise, when she'd craved his smallest gesture. When she'd wanted to be more than the American fortune he'd married. But that time had ended.

"Sham flattery will get you as far as traveling on a one-legged pony would." Which was to say nowhere at all.

"What of truthful flattery?" His thumb kneaded into the taut muscles of her neck in lazy circles. "You're lovely." His breath teased her lips. He'd drawn nearer, near enough to kiss. He leaned forward.

No. She would not allow him to so easily sway her. He didn't deserve her, the knave. "Please don't."

It was too bad, really, that she hadn't realized what he was about, that she'd been so pathetically naïve. He had done his best to court her as though it wasn't her fortune he was after. She knew differently now.

"Don't what?" He came even closer. "Don't do this?" Pembroke lowered his mouth to hers for a slow, soft kiss. He fitted his upper lip between hers, gently at first, and then with increasing pressure, catching her bottom lip between his teeth and tugging. "Or this?" He pulled the bedclothes from her grasp.

She wasn't sure which was worse, his sudden amorous advances after so long a silence or her traitorous reaction to them. He cupped her breasts through the delicate fabric of her nightdress. A slow, languorous ache slid through her, no matter how much she tried to stifle it. Every part of her body reawakened. He'd introduced her to this world of pleasure before shutting her out of it.

"Pembroke," she protested, but her voice was shamefully weak. She loved his hands on her, always had. The awful man knew his way about a woman's body, and though it was plainly the result of far too much carnal knowledge, she couldn't deny the way that particular surfeit of knowledge made her feel. Her nipples hardened.

She forced herself to think of the women whose bedchambers he'd been frequenting during his absence. Their names were a dagger's prick to her senses. *Lady Lonsdale. The Duchess of Eastwick. Mrs. St. Hillaire.*

He grazed her lips with his again, exerting just enough pressure to leave her hungry for more. He knew how to kiss, the devil. "Have you missed me?" he whispered into her mouth.

She swallowed, holding herself stiffly, refusing to capitulate. "Not in the least."

Hadn't there been the Countess of Ardmore, after all? Lady Northclyffe, too. The gossip had been more prolific than a New York blizzard. At first she'd devoured each troubling bit of news. But it had been too painful, and so she'd stopped her connection with the outside world, save letters from her dear friend Maggie in London and her family in New York, who remained blissfully unaware of her husband's peccadillos.

His mouth moved over hers with increasing insistence. He smelled divine. *Lady Shillington. The actress Lillie Longwood.* She bit his lip. Not with enough force to bloody him, but with a pressure that stated her resistance. He could not simply appear in the night and bend her to his whims with his good looks and bone-melting kisses. No, he could not. She was not a twig to bow in the wind of his whims. She was a woman. A woman with a heart and feelings, a woman who'd been cured of the naïveté with which she'd married him.

"Damn it!" He hauled back, staring at her as though she were a creature he'd just witnessed in the wild for the first time. "You bit me."

"Did I?" She kept her tone light, unconcerned. "I'm terribly sorry."

"I detect a notable lack of sincerity." He pressed his fingers to his mouth before holding them out for inspection. "No blood, thank Christ."

She caught the bedclothes in her hand and held them over her bosom as though it were a suit of armor. "I wouldn't dream of disfiguring you. What would all your ladybirds think?"

"Ladybirds." He stared at her, his expression revealing nothing.

Did he think her daft? Well, perhaps she couldn't

entirely blame him for his underestimation of her. After all, she'd been duped by him before, and her stupidity aggrieved her still.

"The women you've been taking to bed," she elaborated. "I won't call them ladies. It's a title they don't deserve, regardless of their ranks."

"I have no ladybirds. Darling, it's you that I want."

The bold pronouncement sent a flurry of old longing through her before she tamped it down. How was it that he could treat her as if she were no more important than a cup of tea and still set her aflame? Thankfully, even if her body and heart were turncoats, her common sense remained. "You cannot expect me to believe such tripe."

"Believe it, love." He squeezed her upper arm. "I've come for you."

He had come to Carrington House, yes. But his intentions weren't as pure as he pretended. Couldn't be. Not after all this time, all this silence. She couldn't help but wonder why, given the intervening months and lack of word, he would appear in her chamber, ready to seduce her as though she were one of his strumpets.

Very well, she'd play at his game. All the better to rout her enemy. "Why now?"

"Why not now?" He gave her another maddening kiss.

She broke it, her palms finding his shoulders and pushing. "Perhaps I ought to rethink your disfigurement. I don't trust you, Pembroke. You're a stranger to me, and I certainly don't want your kisses. Surely there are any number of women scattered about London who would be more than eager to receive them."

"I'm not so strange. I'm your husband." He slid her nightdress down over her shoulder. "And I daresay your lips might be telling me one tale, but your body tells me another. You aren't as cold as you would pretend, my girl."

"You're five months too late recalling we're wed, my lord." How many nights had she lain alone, thinking of his kiss, his hands on her, his body joining hers? Far too many to give in with such ease, her conscience warned her. She did not wish to become a victim to him yet again. "Or do you expect me to believe you've suffered a blow to the head and have been wandering about London an amnesiac left with no choice save pilfering the drawers of every woman you can find?"

He nipped the curve of her shoulder with his teeth, sending a shiver of awareness through her. "On that account, I can assure you that you're hopelessly wrong, my dear. I've never once purloined the drawers of any lady of my acquaintance."

How like him not to deny his sins but to attempt distraction and seduction instead. "That is probably owed to them not wearing any," she said with grim boldness, not caring if she shocked him. Let him be shocked. Let him be angry. Let him be anything but the cad she'd married, all beautiful of face and silver of tongue.

He cast her an amused glance as he licked her skin. "Have you a peculiar habit of peering beneath other ladies' skirts? I daresay if you have, I might be tempted to watch."

The rotten man. She should've known she couldn't shock someone of his reputation, a man who thought he could leave his wife to collect dust in the countryside while he gadded about London, only to return months later with fast hands and a wicked mouth. "Of course I haven't, you scoundrel." She shrugged away from him. "If there is anyone in this chamber with a fondness for being beneath other ladies' skirts, it is you."

"Fair enough. I'll own my failings." He stilled, capturing her gaze with his. Even after all he'd done, the impact took her breath. "I've hurt you."

Pembroke said it as though he were just processing the realization, almost as if the fact that she possessed feelings was a revelation. Perhaps he had never thought of her as a flesh-and-blood woman with expectations and emotions. Certainly, it would have been far more convenient for him that way.

Of course he had hurt her. He'd hurt her far more than she cared to admit and far more than she *would* admit to him. "You disappointed me and misused me."

"I'm sorry, darling." He bent his head and kissed her shoulder again.

She wished that apology hadn't slid so effortlessly off his tongue, for it only underscored his disingenuousness. But she wasn't the girl he'd married any longer, now was she? She had come a long way from the quiet, shy debutante who'd been more terrified of London's Upper Ten Thousand than she'd been of New York's frigid Four Hundred.

Victoria stopped him again. "No. You mustn't."

"Ah, but I must." Her husband's mouth was on her neck, kissing a trail over her bare skin.

She steeled herself against him. His brand of persuasion was exceedingly intoxicating, but the price would prove dear. It always had with him. "When last I saw you, your tone was quite different," she reminded.

"Circumstances change." Somehow, the bedclothes had pooled around her waist once more. He peeled the fabric of her nightdress back and kissed his way down the swell of one breast.

"How could they have changed so swiftly?" She pushed him away but he caught her hands, turning them over to kiss. "You made it abundantly clear you didn't want a wife, and you most certainly didn't want me."

"I did no such thing," he scoffed. His teeth scored the sensitive center line of her palm.

Victoria recalled all too well the awful argument they'd had before he left for London. His words still stung, even with the intervening time that had passed. *I married you because I had no other option besides penury. My father demanded it. I bloody well never wanted a wife. I've done my duty, and now I'm going to carry on living my life as I see fit.*

The Duke of Cranley held Pembroke's purse strings, she had discovered after their nuptials took place. The duke wanted his heir to settle down, and he'd done what he needed to make certain the unruly Pembroke would comply. He'd cut him off. Having satisfied the old man's stipulation, Pembroke had once again had no need for an unwanted wife. He'd left her behind in the country and pretended as if she didn't exist.

She'd somehow been foolish enough to believe he held her in regard, but he had merely been good at manipulation and getting what he wanted. She had begged him to stay, and he'd looked through her as if she were a piece of furniture in his study. Expendable. The reminder was like stepping into a hip bath of ice water. She shoved him. "Go away, Pembroke."

He rolled over onto his back, his big body stretched out alongside hers, and heaved a sigh. "I can't go away. I live here."

"You live in London," she countered.

"I live wherever I choose."

She supposed he did. But he'd chosen to live as far away from her as possible. Victoria straightened her nightdress and propped herself up on her elbow to study him. "Why have you decided to return to Carrington House? Truly?"

He skewered her with a ferocious frown. "Why pepper your husband with blasted questions when he's just returned home? Should you not be overjoyed to see me?"

Victoria considered him, wishing he was not quite so debonair, not quite so compelling. Not quite so likeable in spite of his voluptuary ways. His teasing air and persuasive kisses were like wine. She didn't dare over imbibe. "No. I daresay I ought not to be. If you think you can return here after mostly ignoring me for the entirety of our marriage and expect a warm welcome, you are positively delusional."

"It's only been a fortnight or so."

Oh he was a maddening creature. "It's been five months."

"Dear me. Has it?" The look he directed her way was half sheepish.

And then, like a sudden burst of light in a dark room, it came upon her, the real reason for her husband's return, for his presence in her chamber, his skilled kisses and roaming hands. Her lips tightened and a wave of fury hit her with so much force her body trembled with it. "You've spent the money you received in the marriage settlement, haven't you?"

He frowned. "Of course not."

She didn't believe him. "The duke has cut you off."

"Lower your voice, my girl. You'll have all the miscreants belowstairs prattling about us."

"I am *not* your girl." Her outrage heightened at his blasé tone. "The only miscreant in this house is you, Pembroke. Now leave me to my slumber and find your own chamber. For that matter, go back to London. Surely there are any number of women awaiting you. I don't want you here."

"I daresay you'll change your mind. Let's not make a row of it."

She gritted her teeth and reached for the Dickens volume, holding it aloft in threatening promise. "If you don't get out at once, I'll give your nose another good, hard thwack with *Great Expectations*."

Pembroke rose to a sitting position, raking a hand through his already-disheveled hair. "You wouldn't."

Perhaps she ought to blacken his eye while she was at it. "I most certainly would. Now get out."

chapter two

*W*ell good Christ, this was proving an utter disaster. There was a very real possibility of bodily harm at the hands of his countess, who currently wielded a book of Dickens as though it were a sword with which she could run him through. Not only that, but she presumed to order him about, demanding that he leave this chamber which, by rights, was truly his, along with everything in it.

Along with *her*.

Jesus, the fire-spitting creature before him was not the woman he'd left behind the day after they'd wed. His plan suddenly seemed far more difficult than he'd supposed, for it all had gone straight to Hades the moment he'd stepped into her dark chamber. The quiet young lady he'd known had turned into a book-wielding virago. Perhaps she was even a trifle unhinged. His nose still smarted with the sting of her unexpected blow, and he found it nearly impossible to believe that she'd actually bitten him as though she were a feral dog.

Of course, perhaps he wasn't so unlike a feral dog

himself, for her nip had made him harder than he'd already been. Although she had made every effort to push him away, he didn't mistake her body's reaction to him. Nor did he mistake his to hers.

Tonight, he saw her in a way he hadn't before. He'd caught a glimpse of vulnerability in her unguarded expression before she'd chased it away with scorn. But it had been there, and that fleeting impression hit him square in the gut as he considered her now. She was just a woman, trapped as surely as he, more than a mere pawn in his war against his father.

The realization shook him in a way nothing else had in his admittedly misbegotten thirty years of life. She raised the book higher, as though to somehow menace him, and the action disbanded the spell that had settled over him. He should have gotten good and soused before coming to her. Perhaps he was growing as addled as the duke.

"Bloody hell, woman, put the book down," he ordered. "I'll overlook the first blow and even the bite, but if you attempt to maim me again, I'm afraid my patience for spoiled American girls will be at an end."

But his words only served to rankle her even more. Roses bloomed in her cheeks, her full lips tightening into a grim line. The oddest urge to kiss them back into their natural, pliable shape hit him. *Ridiculous.* He didn't want this woman, this stranger with a gleaming cascade of golden hair falling over her shoulders, with her flat New York accent and freckled, *retroussé* nose. He never had.

In the time he'd been away, his mind had not often flitted to her. It was true what she'd said. *Petite souris*, he'd thought when he'd first seen her in a crushed ballroom, little mouse. His to play with and then abandon at will. It had been dreadfully easy to ply her with charm. Easier still to leave her behind and all but forget her existence as he buried himself in all manner of vices in London.

"Indeed, my lord?" Her voice was frigid as Wenham Lake ice. "How very amusing, for I find that my patience for spoiled English earls who've never known an inkling of responsibility in their misspent lives is at an end as well. That means you really ought to go."

She had cheek, and the perverse streak that had always run through him admired her gumption. But her words had also touched a far more sensitive vein inside him, the one he'd fought for years to dull with hedonistic distraction. *Responsibility. Duty.* They were words he loathed, words that in his youth meant accepting whatever abuse his father had chosen to inflict upon him. *It is your duty as the heir. You have a responsibility.* For a moment, as the past threatened to intrude upon his sanity, he swore he could feel the brutal lash of the last caning he'd received, hear the sick crack of bone. Broken ribs were the devil of a thing.

"Careful, darling," he warned.

She watched him, seemingly weighing her options. The Dickens volume remained aloft, her battle colors flying. "What should I be careful of? What will you do, sir? Will you bed me and then leave? Will you abandon me to rot here for a year? Ten years?"

She had no notion of who he was, of just how low and depraved he could be. And she was foolishly brave to mock him, to tempt the beast within to roar to life. "I'm much larger than you." Keeping his tone even was a struggle. Suddenly, he wanted to grab her by the shoulders and shake her. This should have been easy. Quick. Instead, he'd spent the last half hour attempting to bed her and being routed at every turn. "I could very easily bend you to my whims, my dear. I could take the book from you. I could take *you*, if I chose."

Her nostrils flared, the only indication that his words affected her. "Ah, at last the charm has fled. No more pretty words and roaming hands? If you would force me, my lord, I have no choice." She dropped the book to the floor, and it was one of the heaviest sounds he'd ever heard. Then she settled into a supine position, arms tight to her sides, still as a corpse, staring at the ceiling. "Here you are, my lord. If it pleases you to take what I'm not willing to give, then take it. It's yours, after all. Everything I've ever had is yours now."

Damn it. Damn her, for being the heiress the duke had chosen to replenish the dwindling family coffers, for being yet another unwanted duty foisted upon him, for being outspoken and bold, for taking him to task and making him feel lower than the worst sort of East End criminal. Damn her for making him see her. For making him want her. For making him see the man he'd become.

He grabbed the bedclothes and yanked them to her chin, disgusted with himself. "I'd never force you."

She met his gaze, unflinching. "I'm not spoiled. Nor am I a girl."

No, she wasn't a girl. She was very much a woman. Her body was lush and full in all the proper places. High, heavy breasts. Rounded thighs, trim ankles. She smelled of orris root, and her hair was a revelation. Freed from the dreadful, pastel gowns she'd worn during her Season, she was all woman. All lovely. Perhaps she had been before, and he'd been so blinded by his resentment that he'd failed to notice. He hadn't been her only suitor, after all. But he'd been the heir to a duchy, and he had won her hand.

Yes, he'd won her, and then he'd left her. Little wonder she thought he would ravage her. Jesus, what a bastard he was. It had been easy to blame her when she'd been an afterthought rather than a woman staring at him with haunted eyes.

"My apologies," he blurted, because he didn't know what else to say and because everything he'd imagined—all the meaningless praise and sweet flattery he'd intended to ply her with—had been vanquished by the sight of her lying still on the bed, waiting for him to abuse her.

She stared at him. "Why have you returned?"

Why had he returned? The answer was simple. He'd made a deal with the devil, and the devil had reneged.

"An inkling of responsibility," he repeated her words as he slid from the bed. With the formality of a suitor in a drawing room, he bowed to her. "I shall leave you to your slumber, my lady. Until tomorrow."

Without waiting for her response, he strode to his adjoining chamber, slamming the door at his back. Damn it all to hell. How had he ever imagined this would be straightforward? Nothing about returning to Carrington Hall and the wife he hadn't wanted was. Here he stood, alone in his unprepared chamber, which he generally disliked even when it had been readied for him and which he vastly disliked when it had not.

The room smelled as though it had been sealed up for quite some time. The lamps were lit, but beyond that, nothing was readied. His valet was likely still overseeing the unpacking of his carriage below, and he was left ringing the bell pull for assistance.

His hands shook. Jesus, she'd unnerved him, his wife. She had a name, of course. *Victoria.* He'd never spoken it aloud, had never even thought it until this moment with the sting of self-disgust roiling through him. How little he knew of her. How little attention he'd paid her. She came from a well-known New York family and her father had made a fortune on stocks before sending her to London with an immense dowry. She hadn't been as bold as some of her fellow American heiresses. She had seemed mild of temperament, given to dreadful dresses. Proper and prim, the sort of lady he sought to avoid at house parties and balls.

The sort of lady one might abandon in the country for five months at a time.

Beyond that, he knew nothing. Not nothing, perhaps. He knew she smelled of violets and her hair felt like heavy silk in his fingers. He knew the lush lines of her body. Thinking of her now, her creamy skin and full breasts, the glimpse he'd caught of a pink, erect nipple—made his cock hard all over again. None of it made sense—not his reaction to her, not her transformation, not any damn bit of it. This odd, inconvenient attraction he felt for her was surely the effect of a lack of spirits and a return to his grim ancestral home and all its demons.

After all, he was the Earl of Pembroke, celebrated womanizer and unrepentant rakehell. He preferred fast women who wore bright colors and low décolletages, women who gambled and changed lovers like gowns and had husbands who didn't mind. His father had hand-selected Victoria as his wife, largely for her marriage settlement of half a million pounds. Not a sum to be sneezed at by anyone these days. Will had been given an ultimatum—marry the chit to restore the familial coffers or be disinherited altogether. He'd swallowed his pride and half a bottle of whisky and made a deal with the devil. Marriage to the little American mouse, then he'd return to his old life once more. And return to his old life he had, with the abandon of the truly dissolute.

Until the summons.

The duke expected him to produce heirs and was not pleased to see his august decree so openly flouted. But Will couldn't resist perturbing the old bastard with a good scandal. He'd allowed Maria to live in the Belgravia townhouse for two months, and she'd destroyed a number of costly family paintings when he'd informed her that her services would no longer be required.

He'd only succeeded in goading his father too far, however. Once again, the duke had been enraged, and when enraged, he issued threats. He'd sworn to take this moldy heap of family stones back into his care—not that Will particularly gave a damn about it. Carrington House had been neglected and virtually abandoned since his mother had died within its walls, and it held few fond memories for him. But this time, the duke had vowed to do away with his entire inheritance save the entail and had immediately cut off all access to further funds until Will finished his duty and provided the duchy with a proper heir.

A man with no blunt was not a man about town.

Which meant returning to his shy mouse of a wife and bedding her until the deed was well and truly done. He'd imagined the naïf he'd left behind to be awaiting him. He hadn't precisely envisioned being attacked by a volume of Dickens, or being so affected by the sight of his wife *en dishabille*, angry color in her cheeks. Or being so affected by his own bloody shortcomings.

A sneeze interrupted his frustrated musings. Good Lord, was that dust he spied on his *Louis Quinze* chair? Where the devil was his valet, anyway? With a sigh of long-suffering impatience, he crossed the chamber and gave the bell pull another forceful yank. He wanted his bed prepared, damn it. He'd traveled all evening and he was tired, and his wife had thrown him out of her sweet-smelling, comfortable high tester.

This was not going to do, none of it. He'd be back in her bed before week's end, he vowed. And before the month was through, she'd be with child and his time of reluctant duty to his father and the great Cranley duchy would be at an end.

He sneezed yet again. Jesus, it couldn't happen soon enough.

Her husband had returned.

This knowledge brought Victoria no comfort as she sat for her morning ritual of chocolate and correspondence. Her hands were unsteady as she perused her customary stack of letters. Some from her sisters. One from her mother. She longed for news from home, but it would only make her weak. And she could not afford to be weak now as she faced Pembroke. He had returned for her, he'd said.

I could very easily bend you to my whims, my dear.

His voice had been low and deceptively calm when he'd issued the warning. She thought of his expression, that of a man torn. Something had brought him back to her side, back to her chamber. That something was not her, no matter how much he pretended it was.

I could take you, if I chose.

She shivered, though somehow those words didn't fill her with trepidation or disgust. What was it that she felt, this awful, unfurling coil deep within? Surely not excitement or a stirring of her old feelings for him. Certainly not desire.

No. He could not take her. She wouldn't allow it. She wasn't so weak, so swayed by his lovemaking. Victoria spied the familiar penmanship of her dear childhood friend Maggie, Marchioness of Sandhurst, and slid the envelope open. They'd grown up together in New York and had landed on England's shores as dollar princesses, as the press had dubbed them. Together, they had navigated the complex terrain of English polite society. It had oft proved more treacherous than the most dangerous passage across the Atlantic ever could.

Maggie's words swirled beneath her eyes now, blurred by a combination of anger and tears. *How dare he?* Had he not already treated her poorly enough? A fresh onslaught of betrayal hit her like a runaway carriage. The letter dropped from her numb fingers and she yanked the bell pull.

She scarcely even paid attention to her *toilette* as she dressed with the help of her lady's maid in unusual speed. By the time she marched into the breakfast room with the letter in hand, she had worked herself into a fine fury.

Pembroke stood at her entrance. He was irritatingly perfect, his well-tailored clothing immaculate, handsome as ever. The utter cad. What right did he have to invade her territory, to make butterflies flit through her stomach even though she knew him for the heartless rake he was? How had he been so brazen to come to her last night, to touch her, to warn her that she was his? She would never, ever be his. What he'd done was beyond the pale.

"Good morning, my lady," he greeted with his standard charm. He scarcely resembled the semi-wild man she'd seen just before he'd stalked to his chamber last night. This Pembroke was collected. Polished. Cheerful, even.

Victoria ignored him and politely dismissed Wilton, the

efficient butler she'd grown to admire over her time at Carrington House. When they were alone, she strode to him, pressing Maggie's carefully worded missive into his hard chest. "Perhaps you would care to read this."

He took the letter from her to scan the contents. "The Marchioness of Sandhurst is a damned meddlesome gossip," he pronounced. "You ought not to know her."

That was all he offered? No apologies, no explanation. Not even an attempt to dissemble. Merely an insult for dear, sweet Maggie while he was the worst creature she'd ever had the misfortune to meet. Where was *Great Expectations* to be found when one needed a weapon with which to knock sense into one's blackguard of a husband? Perhaps she could dump his plate of breakfast into his lap.

She gritted her teeth. "That is all you have to say for yourself?"

"Need I say more? I feel confident my opinion of Lady Sandhurst is quite warranted."

The arrogance of the man. She'd had enough. To hell with the breakfast in his lap. Before she even knew what she was about, she slapped him. The satisfying sound of her palm connecting with his face echoed in the silence.

He rubbed his jaw, watching her like a hunter intent upon his prey. The mild disinterest vanished, replaced by something indefinably dangerous. "Do you not think you're being a tad dramatic, my dear?"

"You allowed your…" She paused and closed her eyes, unable to say the word "mistress" aloud. Ladybird she could say in a fit of pique. Mistress was something far more intimate, as it implied a favored status. A permanent relationship to rival the marriage itself, in some instances. Her mother had told her never to acknowledge such a thing existed, and for the entirety of her marriage to Pembroke she had not. She had not while whispers inevitably made their way to her. She had pretended to be unaware, had pretended not to care. But this was the outside of enough.

"Signora Rosignoli," he supplied.

Her eyes flew open, her entire body shaking with roiling emotion. "You dare to speak her name?"

Pembroke raised an imperious brow. "What would you have me call her?"

She had tolerated his abandonment. She had quietly accepted gossip sheets and Maggie's letters about her husband carrying on with widows and lonely wives, had pretended each new name hadn't scored another wound in her heart. But this, she was quite certain, was beyond the pale. He had openly lived with a courtesan, opera singer or no, and had done so for all the world to know. He had touched the woman, kissed her, allowed her to dwell in the family house as recently as a fortnight ago. Last night, he had come to Victoria claiming he wanted to atone for his sins. It would have been laughable if the notion of this *Signora Rosignoli* in his bed didn't make her ill. And still he dared to view it all with a carelessness that made her long to slap him once more.

She took a deep breath, her corset nipping at her sides. "Never again speak of her to me."

He shrugged. "It will be as you wish."

A physical ache took up residence in her breast. She didn't know whether to cry or rage. She wished she had never consented to marry him. She wished to God she had become a spinster and gone back to the city she loved and so dearly missed. At least her life had not been a mockery in New York, with no one to hurt her.

Her vision grew dark around the edges as if she were about to swoon. She needed to escape. How had she been naïve enough to allow him to kiss her last night? How weak she'd been. Worse, she had enjoyed his mouth, his touch.

"This marriage has become insupportable to me," she said on a rush.

He calmly turned back to the table as though she hadn't said a word. "I recommend you collect yourself and enjoy breakfast with me."

Did he truly think there would be no consequences for

his actions? That she would sit and eat kippers and toast as if nothing untoward had occurred? As if she had not just discovered the depths of his depravity and duplicity? True, she was at his mercy as his wife. He could carry on as he wished with every opera singer and unscrupulous lady he liked, and he could keep her in the country, and he could use all of her money to buy dresses and baubles for his conquests. She had no rights. Indeed, she had less rights than an unmarried female.

But that did not mean she would calmly lie down for slaughter. "I don't care what you recommend, Pembroke. I may be subject to your whims, but know that you disgust me."

He smiled but it did little to relieve the harsh planes of his brooding expression. "I believe I've already disproved your claim."

She gasped, shocked that even he would stoop to such a level. "How dare you?"

Pembroke gave another shrug. "Why bother with deceit?"

"I daresay deceit is all you've been bothering yourself with, my lord."

"You go too far," he warned, standing at last.

He towered over her diminutive stature, but she didn't care. "It is you who has gone too far. Was it not cruel enough to discard me as if I were no better than an outmoded waistcoat? Now you come to me in lies and try to make love to me as if you actually had a care for me when all along it was a farce. Did you laugh to yourself, thinking you made me the fool once again? Tell me, did you crow with all your friends at how you'd hie off to the country and make me your dupe again? Did you even think about me when you were living with your paramour?"

She didn't need an answer to her questions for she already knew. Of course he had not thought of her. Very likely, he never thought of her at all. She envisioned a gloriously beautiful woman with dark hair and a voluptuous figure lounging about in his bed and revulsion swept over her. Of course his mistress would be ravishing. She wondered if he kissed and caressed Signora Rosignoli the way he had touched her last night.

Pembroke closed the distance between them with one angry stride and caught her against him, trapping her in his arms. "Stop this nonsense, Victoria. I'll not hear another word of it."

She was in no mood to be subdued. She struck out at his chest with her fists, wanting to pummel him. "Then you shall have to sew my mouth shut, you rotten cad."

"Or I shall have to kiss your mouth shut."

His mouth was sudden and hard, almost bruising over hers. Angry as she was, her body still responded to him, and she loathed it and him both. His chest was muscled and tempting. He didn't live an idle life, not from the feel of things. But that just reminded her how little she knew of him. He'd been living apart from her for nearly half a year. His tongue swept over the seam of her lips then, seeking to plunder and render her mindless.

But Victoria was determined not to give in to him this time. She pushed him away. "Lovemaking is not a cure, Pembroke."

He gave her a wry grin. "Perhaps it is a symptom then."

She studied his eyes, unable to fathom his thoughts. "A symptom of what?"

"Of being a rotten cad." He took her hands in his. "We are husband and wife. We cannot forever be at odds."

"Your actions have proven otherwise to me." She tried to escape from his touch but he was persistent and stronger. "I understand you do not care for me, and I never cared for you. I never wish to ever be in your presence again."

"Victoria." He gripped her waist and pulled her into his tall, lean body, anchoring her against him. He lowered his head until their noses nearly bumped. His breath was a hot, invisible curtain drawing over her lips.

Despite her anger and disillusionment, she was

breathless, caught in his smoldering gaze. "I think that I hate you," she whispered. She hated him as much for what he had done as the way he made her feel. Dizzy, confused, hopelessly wanting. How could she want such an unfeeling rake? What had he ever done but lie to her and manipulate her to suit his own interests? And yet his mouth on hers made her shamefully vulnerable.

"Before you can hate someone, you must have loved them first," he said, his eyes dropping to her mouth.

She tried to squelch the rampant stirring of desire his nearness and heated glances produced. "You speak like a man who has learned from experience," she observed.

He shook his head slowly. "I have never loved anyone."

She supposed she shouldn't be disappointed to have final confirmation that he'd never harbored a tender feeling toward her. But the revelation still stung. Surely he must have loved someone at some point in his life?

"Not your mother?"

His expression was impassive as ever. "My mother only had time for balls and lovers. What was there to love?"

"Your father the duke then," she suggested, thinking of the rigid, silver-haired man she had met on only a handful of occasions. His demeanor was hopelessly grim and disapproving at all times, it seemed.

"I neither hate him nor love him." Pembroke's beautiful mouth drew into a sneer. "I feel nothing for the man. My hatred would give him power, and I refuse to give him anything."

She was once more baffled. "How can you feel nothing? He's your blood, your family."

He met her gaze. "Family means little to those who easily betray it. He has not inspired anything in me other than a desire to be the thorn in the lion's paw."

Something must have happened between the duke and her husband. Pembroke surely lied when he said he felt nothing. It seemed odd indeed that she would have been married to the earl for so many months while so much of his life remained unknown to her. She had to believe there was a reason behind his lack of faith.

Or perhaps that was her heart wanting to believe. Focusing her thoughts proved difficult while trapped in the seductive spell cast by being in his arms. It would not do. She'd finally found her strength, and she couldn't abandon it now.

She gathered up her courage to say what she'd decided she must. "I don't want to be married to you any longer, Pembroke."

He stilled, his hands tightening on her cinched waist. "I beg your pardon?"

He seemed genuinely aghast. Victoria felt the heat of his large hands even through the French silk of her day gown, the layers of her undergarments, and the stiffness of her corset. Dear heavens, she wished she was not so drawn to him.

"I no longer wish to be your wife," she elaborated, her voice as pinched as her waist felt.

"I'm afraid you're a bit tardy in that realization, my dear. We're irrevocably wed. We've consummated our union." His gaze was scorching upon her. "Surely you haven't forgotten? The law has strict requirements in these matters."

Oh he was a wilier opponent than she had realized. He knew all too well that mentioning the consummation of their marriage would bring with it an onslaught of memories. Pleasurable memories. She'd had no complaints in her marriage bed other than that her husband had disappeared from it and chosen to share it with others instead. She could not forget his sins, particularly after he had flaunted it by living with that woman.

"You abandoned me," she pointed out, "and I have ample proof of adultery."

"Complete shite," he said. "Everyone knows divorce is only granted when one of the parties is a fair candidate for the lunatic asylum. More importantly, how can I have abandoned you when I've returned?"

It was true that divorce was rarely granted, particularly in the English aristocracy. Indeed, seeking divorce was seldom attempted for the dreadful fall from grace that ensued. Husbands and wives could do as they wished in seeking bed partners as long as the scandal was not too great. It was Victoria's experience that the Marlborough House Set, including the prince himself, made adultery into a sport. She simply hadn't realized she'd been marrying a man who subscribed to the same belief. She had not taken her vows lightly, despite the financially motivated underpinnings of their union.

The way he held her in his arms now could not sway her. Must not sway her.

"I want a divorce," she said with quiet force.

His mouth flattened. "Preposterous, if not altogether impossible."

"You don't want a wife," she pointed out, trying to wrestle away from his grasp without success.

"I do." He feathered a light kiss over her lips. "I've come back to Carrington House because I want to start anew."

She didn't want to enjoy his kiss, especially now that word of his opera singer had made his betrayal all too real. But the plain truth was that she did. His lips on hers sent desire through her. She wanted him in an elemental sense. That much she could not deny.

The truth slipped from her lips before she could hold it back and protect herself. "Pray do not prevaricate any longer. It hurts me too much."

Hell.

He didn't want to hurt her. That was a new sensation for him, caring. Ordinarily, he was damn good at not having a care. He'd made a life out of it, at any rate. But his wife had donned a silken dress that showed off the very curves he'd spent the night recalling, and her breasts were a luscious temptation against his chest. His cock was rigid in his trousers, a reminder that despite the vagaries of their situation, he truly did want her.

Still, it wasn't just lust that sliced straight through his gut at her admission, was it? No, it was something more, something indefinable yet powerful. She wasn't biting or walloping him now. She was sincere, her stricken eyes telling him more than her words could. And this time, he didn't want to use her. Couldn't bear it, actually. The mere thought filled him with disgust for the way he'd treated her.

He hadn't been prepared to desire her this much. Or to feel compassion for her. Last night had not been an irregularity, for he felt just as raw now as he had then. It was unsettling, to say the least. Damn if he didn't like her scent more than Maria's preferred French rose. Here in the brash morning light, he saw her uncolored by the resentment and anger that tainted his every interaction with his father.

She had asked him not to lie to her any longer. But if he told her the real reason for his return, she'd leave him for certain, ruining any chance he had to produce an heir. He couldn't afford to lose everything. He had no doubt his father would leave him destitute. The entail was very insignificant at this point, a mere few thousand pounds a year and Carrington House. Thanks to the marriage settlement orchestrated by the old miser duke, the bulk of Victoria's substantial dowry had been left in the care of his father, out of Will's reach. While a stipulated sum had been set aside specifically for Carrington House, it was to be kept in trust by the duke, doled out as he saw fit. He was at his father's mercy just as he had been his entire life.

Little wonder he had resented her. She'd been one more ducal edict he was forced to obey. The day after they'd wed, he'd been so desperate to flee her, the symbol of everything he hated about himself, that he'd simply left. But now he noticed her, damn it all. She was clever and bold, capable and kind. The servants of Carrington House had been singing her praises at every opportunity. Even he, blind fool that he was, could see the changes she'd brought about while he'd left her to dally in London. She'd been constant. She hadn't taken lovers. Not a hint of scandal darkened her name. In fact, she was a paragon. A lovely paragon who wore her heart on her sleeve, who'd effortlessly turned the family ruins into a gleaming, improved version of its former self. Even the carpet was new.

But to hell with carpet. Her lips were his for the taking.

He kissed her rather than making any admissions. It seemed easier. He was good at lovemaking—he'd spent years honing his craft. She tasted like chocolate. Her mouth opened for him at last, and he swept his tongue inside, hungry for more of her. He slid his palm up her back, the sensation of her fine silk against his traveling hand tantalizing him. His other hand traced her wasp-like waist before lingering over her breast.

Suddenly, his desire accelerated from a flame into a more uncontrollable fire. He hadn't bedded a woman in some time. Maria had bored him, and if he were honest, he'd only been using her as a means of infuriating the duke. What he felt for Victoria was somehow new and incredibly potent.

Groaning into her mouth, he led her backward until her derriere rested on the edge of the breakfast table. He reached around her, trying but failing to find her bottom in the elaborate pinning of fabric at the back of her skirts. Instead, he lifted her and settled her upon the table. She was deuced small compared to him, her head scarcely reaching his chest. Her new position allowed him better access.

He dragged his mouth down her throat, finding it soft and creamy white. A high, stiff collar with a small bow stopped him from exploring her décolletage as he wanted. Damn women's peculiar fashions. He cupped her breast, jealous of her corset. Her bosom was perfection, high and firm and begging to be admired.

"Pembroke." Victoria's throaty murmur cut into his passion-hazed thoughts, an unwanted interruption.

"What is it, my dear?" He licked a path to her ear, then

caught her lobe in his teeth for a gentle nibble.

"You cannot erase what's happened with kisses." She placed staying palms on his shoulders.

He permitted her to put some space between them, even though his body cried out at the denial. "I don't seek to erase," he said with the most honesty he'd given her since his return. "I seek a new beginning." Because he had to win her over or face the consequences. But maybe, just maybe, for other reasons that he didn't care to examine as well.

"I don't think I can let you," she whispered, her small, heart-shaped face cast with a stricken expression.

Why had he never noticed the vivid green of her eyes? It was like staring into the grass in spring, bright and precious after a cruel winter. Her lips were red with his kisses, too large for fashion but nevertheless inviting. Her golden hair had been tricked into an elaborate coiffure he wanted to undo. Last night, he'd sworn her curls had gone to her waist. She was stunning.

He looked at her as if he were seeing her for the first time, and mayhap he was. *Petite souris*. It didn't fit—it had never fit. She wasn't at all plain. She wasn't a typical English beauty, true. But she was lovely in a way that was patently hers, and he wanted to bed her with an irrational need. Perhaps it was because she was denying him. Perhaps it was because she was different than he remembered, showing him such fire. She was his, and yet he didn't deserve her. He didn't know why he wanted her with such unexpected desperation, though with the insistent hardness of his cock, he was sure he didn't care. When he fucked, he wasn't required to think. He didn't need to recall just how much of a bastard he'd been to the woman in his arms. How appallingly much like his father.

"You can let me, my dear. I'm your husband," he cajoled, giving her another sound kiss. He could lose himself in her, spend inside her, forget everything and everyone as he made her body sing with pleasure.

She kissed him in return, her arms going round his neck.

She fitted her lips to his with an unpracticed urgency that ensnared him. He thought he was gaining ground until she stopped, tearing her mouth away. Her eyes were wide and expressive. "I cannot. You don't understand, Pembroke. It's too difficult." She pushed at him again and he moved, although the force she exerted wasn't enough to move a baby rabbit.

Victoria hopped down from the table, her breathing visibly heavy. Her expression was nearly indecipherable, but perhaps a combination of agony and longing. He hoped for the longing, at least. The rest of his life depended upon it.

Mayhap even the rest of their life together, if there could indeed be such a thing.

"I will prove myself to you," he vowed, though he hadn't the slightest notion of how he could accomplish such a feat. After all, he had no choice. He never had.

chapter three

Victoria hovered at the threshold of the music room, watching Pembroke's broad back as he played. Faint strains of piano music had drifted to her in the library. Lively and lilting, the tune had drawn her from her hiding place among the musty walls of books. She'd known, of course, that it was him playing. Surely no servant would dare to make a presumption so glaring, and surely no servant could play with such practiced skill. But still she'd come, her curiosity luring her.

The thought of him playing an instrument, creating the haunting beauty of a melody, those long fingers of his working over the keys, had somehow seemed impossible. Improbable. For no man could play the piano as he did— with effortless beauty and striking passion—without possessing a soul. And up until this very moment, she would've sworn he didn't have one.

She caught her skirts in her hand. Truly, she should go before he caught sight of her. Spending time alone with Pembroke, she'd fast discovered, was perilous to her newfound sense of liberty. She'd realized something about herself since his return. For all that she'd felt trapped in the country, she'd delighted in her task of making Carrington House shine again. Even the piano he played, the room in which he set loose such passionate notes, had been in sad neglect. She'd had the piano tuned and ebonized, the room dusted and rearranged, the stained wallpaper, worn carpets, and outmoded furniture replaced. Her father had sent her a handsome allotment, and she'd put those funds to good use.

Yes, she really ought to go. The song, a familiar tune by Pleyel, was nearing its completion. At any moment, he could turn, catch sight of her, attempt to importune her again with sinful kisses and a wandering touch. Of course she didn't want that. She turned.

The music stopped, the air going still.

"Wait."

Ignore him. Just go. Keep walking. She took another step, self-preservation at the reins.

"Victoria, don't go."

She pivoted before she could rethink the wisdom of obeying him. His words had been part demand, part request. He didn't deserve her presence. She didn't owe him her time. But their gazes clashed and held, and even with the distance between them, something made her retrace her steps, at least back to the threshold where she'd lingered before.

"What do you want, my lord?" She would be cool to him. Civil but not kind. Above all, she didn't owe him kindness.

He stood, and she realized for the first time how informally he was dressed. Trousers and a crisp white shirt beneath a charcoal waistcoat. No jacket. He looked at home, and the thought produced an unwanted frisson of emotion unfurling within her.

"Do you intend to hover in the hall, or will you join me?"

His rakish grin, taunting and yet inviting, sent heat careening through her. "I intend to remain where I'm safe."

"Ah." He sauntered toward her with the bold air of a

man who knew exactly the picture he presented. Who knew exactly how much he could make a woman—any woman—want him. "You speak of yesterday's breakfast."

"I speak of your attempts to sway me from my course." Divorce. Yes, that was her course. Even if she had brokered a sort of peace for herself here, a certain amount of contentedness cultivated by her industrious nature, Carrington House was not where she belonged. England was not where she belonged. Nor was she meant to be his wife.

He stopped when he was near enough that her skirts brushed his trousers. His expression was unreadable. "Your course? Surely you cannot be continuing on with this divorce claptrap?"

How dare he dismiss her concerns, he who had spent all of their married life chasing other women until a scant few days ago? Her lips flattened into a grim line. "Freedom is not claptrap, my lord."

"Freedom." He caught her chin between his thumb and forefinger, tipping it up. "Freedom is an American fiction. Of course you must realize that none of us, neither you nor I, are ever truly free, Lady Pembroke. The whims of society and the trappings of our civilized world see to that."

She pulled away from his grasp. "What a grim view of the world you must have."

He smiled at that, but it was not a smile that carried to the vivid depths of his blue eyes. Nor was it particularly pleasant. "Surely no more grim than your view of me, dear heart."

Victoria swallowed. Was it just her imagination, or was he leaning into her? Her skirts hadn't been so thoroughly crushed against his powerful thighs just a moment ago, had they? She didn't dare look down or glance away. He was an odd, compelling man, at turns charming and carefree, others dark and jaded. Perhaps the real Pembroke could be found somewhere in between the disparate faces he presented.

"You haven't given me reason to view you otherwise,"

she pointed out to him.

"I shall endeavor to change that."

"You needn't bother."

He stared at her, long and frank, until her cheeks heated. "Why don't you cross the threshold? I rather fancy you don't trust yourself."

She scoffed. "Of course I trust myself. It is you I don't trust. It is you who isn't *worthy* of my trust."

"Can it be that you're afraid?" he drawled the question, almost as if he were bored. But his expression told a far different tale. He was intent. Intent upon her.

"Don't be foolish." She whirled past him, stalking into the music room and twirling in a melodramatic circle before she could think of how silly it must make her look. Spinning about for the Earl of Pembroke? What in heaven's name was the matter with her? She stopped, facing him, uncertain of what to say next. "Here I am. Unafraid."

"Here you are," he agreed calmly, striding toward her, eating up the space she'd just so breezily put between them. He caught her around the waist, drawing her suddenly up against his tall, hard body. "Here you are."

Her hands fluttered up, her palms pressing to his shoulders, and she instantly wished she hadn't touched him at all. He was so very warm through his shirtsleeves. So vital. His scent drifted over her. Musk and shaving soap. She forced herself to think of anything else. "You play quite well, my lord."

"I'd forgotten how good it felt," he startled her by saying. His hands splayed over her waist in a possessive grip. Part of her relished it. Another part of her was horrified by it. "There is something about losing one's self that is quite heady." His head dipped lower, his breath fanning over her lips.

Oh dear. She had sworn she would not again wind up in such a position, at his mercy. As his willing dupe. "I didn't know you favored the piano," she said stupidly. But it was true. She hadn't. This music room had been meant for her, not for him. That they stood in it together now seemed almost surreal.

"There are a great many things you don't know about me." One of his hands slid up her back to tangle in the hair at her nape. His fingers flexed, catching in the strands. "Just as there are many things I don't know about you. I want to learn, Victoria. I want to learn *you*."

"It's too late for that." Even if his bold proclamation did create a pang in her heart that echoed the pulse of need growing elsewhere.

His gaze dropped to her mouth, and she felt it like a kiss. "Are you certain, my dear? It doesn't feel too late to me."

"It felt too late to me the moment you left for London," she snapped, holding fast to her frustration, her anger. It was the only shield she had remaining, for her body was about to become limp and pliant and eager in his hands.

"I'm here now." He caught her hand and pressed it to his chest, just above his thumping heart.

She tried to twist away from his grasp, but he refused to allow her retreat, holding her still. *Thump, thump, thump* went his heart. Such a visceral reminder that he was only a man, after all. "You're here until you get whatever it is you've come for."

He shook his head slowly. "I've already told you what I'm here for, my dear. I've come for you."

The Lord must have had a laugh when he bestowed that beautiful face on such a rotter of a man, she thought. That face was inconstant. Untrustworthy. That face was faithless. Fathomless. She looked away, staring at the striped wallpaper. "You think me a fool, then. Is that it?" Her eyes flew back to him and she made another failed attempt to snatch back her hand. "Does it entertain you to win me and abandon me for a second time?"

He released her hand. "And yet you were just spouting of freedom and divorce, my lady. Tell me, which is it? Do you wish me here or do you wish to leave me?"

Her face flamed in embarrassment, for he was right. The

truth of it was, she didn't know what she wanted, not any longer. Not as her husband plied her with charm, holding her in his strong embrace. Not as his mouth lingered so near to hers. Not as every bit of her clamored for more. Her body responded to him now as it always had, and her weakness was a devil of a thing.

"I want a divorce," she said softly. "I want to return to New York. You are unencumbered by me. Go back to London and your beautiful Signora."

His mouth hardened. "I don't want you in New York, damn it. I want you here where you belong."

How did he dare to think that what he wanted was of any consequence to her? "I don't belong here. I never did."

"Tell me, what has changed? All this time, no one was holding you here against your will. You could have gone back to New York a dozen times by now, and yet you stayed. You redecorated the music room and tuned the piano. And here you are, in my arms."

She didn't want to think about the last five months, about how she'd agonized, torn between hurt and anger, duty and indifference, fear and indecision. Longing and resentment. "Someone needed to care for this place and these people."

"It needn't have been you, my lady, and yet you remained." He held up his hands between them like a supplicant. "Even now, you could push away from me at any time. I'll not stop you. Walk away."

What a terrible, shameful shock to realize that it was *she* who held him now, one hand still above his steadily beating heart, the other on his shoulder. He'd drawn her into his web in true spider fashion.

She extricated herself as quickly as if he were made of flame, pushing him away from her. "Don't you dare toy with me. Have you not already done enough? Are you not satisfied?"

"Walk away, Victoria." His expression had grown hard. "Walk away before I do something we'll both regret."

The old bitterness cut through her. "It would merely be one more in a vast ocean of them. Go ahead. Do your worst."

He caught her arms in a punishing grip, spun her around, and pressed her back to the wall of the music room. His mouth came down on hers, hungry and demanding.

He kissed her with the fury and tumult raging through him. Will was angry with himself, angry with her, angry at the position in which he found himself. *Freedom is not claptrap*, she'd said with her naïve American ideals. There was no freedom, not for either of them. There never would be. They were inescapably trapped by their union, by duty, the duke, society. Damn it all to hell. Damn everything and everyone but this.

Her.

His tongue sank into her mouth, tasting, claiming, seeking. He cupped her face, his fingers sinking back into the soft cloud of her hair. Too many pins, too many coils. He plucked the pins free, wanting to see her long, burnished curls by the light of day, hanging to her waist. He caught the fullness of her lower lip between his teeth, needing to consume her. She tasted of bergamot and honey.

She clutched at him, and he didn't know if she intended to push him away or pull him closer, but she made no move to protest. She wanted him, even if her wounded pride wouldn't allow her to admit it. Her hair had come unbound now, heavy waves spilling down her shoulders and back.

He broke the kiss and stared down into her upturned face. The green of her eyes was especially vivid, her lush mouth swollen. *There.* Proper progress. He tested the unruly skeins of her hair, letting it sift through his fingers. With his other hand, he caught her chin, swiping the pad of his thumb over her parted lips. The freckles on her nose beckoned. He kissed them and just barely refrained from licking them as though they were tiny specks of sugar on her skin.

Jesus, what was wrong with him? Was he depraved? He wasn't supposed to be enjoying this. He needn't seduce her. All that was required of him was an heir. A quick coupling and a spend. But he couldn't stop. Didn't, in fact, want to stop. For now, he was kissing her neck, nibbling at the sensitive cords where her pulse told him she was every bit as affected as he.

Some darkness inside him made him long to rattle her. No, he bloody well was not going to stop until he had her precisely where he wanted her. She could only hold on to her anger for so long. He knew how to dismantle any woman's defenses. No one was immune. Not even the wife-turned-temptress in his arms.

He sucked her earlobe, found the hollow behind her ear with his tongue and tasted violets. She moaned his title. *Pembroke.* A sigh. A spurring plea. He'd never been so aroused by the sound of his name on a woman's tongue.

"Yes, darling," he murmured against her skin as he gave her little nips and soothing kisses. He caught her lace and silk skirts, dragging them upward. His hand traveled from the curve of her knee to the tie of her stockings, then higher. "I warned you to walk away, but you didn't. Now you have to pay the price."

He licked behind her ear again, the spot that was driving her mad, just as he nudged her thighs apart and found the slit of her drawers. Hot, slick flesh welcomed him in. He circled her pearl and worked the engorged nub gently at first and then with increasing pressure as she pressed into him.

She cried out. He slid a finger inside her. Ah, Christ. She was hot and tight, and suddenly he couldn't be deep enough, couldn't have as much as he needed. He had to taste her. He sank to his knees, holding the flounces of her skirt to her waist. For a moment, he took in her petite ankles and well-shaped calves encased in silk, and then he saw only the erotic sight of his hand disappearing in the opening of her drawers. He teased a second finger inside, curving it to intensify her pleasure.

"Hold your skirts," he ordered her, not wanting to be encumbered by the heavy impediment. All of his focus, all of his energy was about to be devoted to one task: making her come. This was how he would win her. This was how he would break her.

"You must stop," she protested, but her tone was weak and breathless, and she made no move to curtail him.

"I'm going to put my tongue on you, inside you." He met her gaze, withdrawing his fingers almost completely before thrusting them back inside and wringing another moan from her, another buck of her hips. "Hold your bloody skirts, darling."

Her eyes went wide. He'd shocked her with his boldness, but he'd also intrigued her. There was no mistaking it. Her hand fisted in her skirts, holding them in place. At last, he thought, his mind half mad with the urge to claim her. *At last.*

He withdrew from her long enough to unbutton the waistband of her drawers and yank them down over her hips. He guided her left knee over his shoulder, cupped the warm swell of her derriere, and sucked her into his mouth. She jerked, her skirts slipping down to rest on his head, but he didn't mind. His tongue explored her, learning her. He ran it beneath her pearl and then gave her a gentle tug with his teeth. So sweet. Sweeter than honey. More. He wanted more.

He licked her seam and then pressed deeper, inside her. Wet. Divine. Delicious. This woman was his, his in a way no other in the world would ever be. His and he would prove it to her. He would brand her, take her higher than she'd dared to imagine. He replaced his tongue with his fingers and sucked her again. Her skirts fell over his head entirely, enveloping him in darkness, but it somehow only heightened his arousal. There was only her scent, earthy and floral, the secrets of her body to savor. She surrounded him.

She consumed him.

Her orgasm was sudden and violent when it came. She shuddered, tightening on his fingers, her wetness dripping warmly down his hand. He didn't stop licking, sucking, and thrusting, drawing out her spend, making it last as long as possible until she wilted against him. With shaking hands, he pulled her drawers back into place, re-buttoning them before he emerged from her skirts. He remained on his knees, his mouth slick with her essence, forcing her to meet his gaze.

She pressed a hand to her mouth, looking stricken, as though she couldn't believe what she'd just allowed him to do to her. Her emerald eyes were wide. For the first time since his return, she was speechless. Very well. He collected the jagged ends of his thoughts—shattered by the sheer bliss of bringing her to her pinnacle—and forced them into a semblance of order.

"I won't stop the next time, Victoria." The words were torn from him, part promise, part warning. But she ought to know who he was. Let her not be fooled again. "I won't stop until I have you beneath me, and I'm sliding my cock so deep inside you that you come undone a hundred times harder than you just did with my fingers and tongue."

Her cheeks went crimson. Making a strangled sound, she spun on her heel and fled the chamber, the door slamming at her back.

Yes, he was depraved. Even more depraved than he'd ever supposed, for he was enjoying this game they played. But he would enjoy winning it even more.

chapter four

*I*T SEEMED UNSEASONABLY WARM AS VICTORIA wandered about in the gardens, even for summer, sun beating upon the pathway she walked. The heady scent of roses in bloom wafted to her. She would, she thought with a touch of sadness, miss this vast estate and its old world beauty. But the time had come for her to leave.

She feared she could no longer remain at Carrington House as long as her husband insisted upon taking up residence there. Oh, the wicked things he had done to her body! She'd known he was a hedonist, but when he'd used his tongue on her, he had proven it tenfold. It had been sinful. Shameful.

Wonderful.

She'd thoroughly enjoyed every second of it, much to her eternal embarrassment. But Victoria considered herself a practical person, and there was no sense in denying the truth. She had liked what her husband had done to her. She'd reveled in it. If she gave him another opportunity, she very much doubted she'd be able to deny him what he'd promised to take.

All of her. She shivered now despite the heat of the day, recalling his words. *I won't stop the next time.* Dear heavens, never mind that. She wouldn't wish him to stop. Something had clearly addled her mind, but the part of her that was rational and reasonable still remained.

She didn't want to give him the opportunity to cause her any further hurt and humiliation. She couldn't trust him, no matter how effortlessly he had unlocked all the mysteries of her body, showing her what she enjoyed on an elemental level. No. She couldn't allow him to make a fool of her again. If he didn't wish to return to London, she would in his stead. It was decided, the servants already going about the task of packing for the trip.

The only glaring trouble with her resolution was that she had yet to inform Pembroke.

A heaviness settled in her heart as she paced. Carrington House's elaborate gardens were one of the few things that had given her life as the Countess of Pembroke a sense of purpose. When she'd arrived, they had been dreadfully in need of care, despite the admirable work of the estate's capable Head Gardener. His focus had been more put upon the fresh vegetables and fruits grown to be sent up to the London townhouse. She took great satisfaction in admiring the beauty produced by her efforts, but today those efforts were lost upon her.

The crunching of gravel startled her, interrupting her musings. She turned to see her husband round the bend, stalking in her direction. He wore trousers and a plain coat with no neckcloth, almost as though he hadn't finished dressing. His expression was thunderous.

Oh dear. Perhaps he'd somehow caught wind of her plans.

He didn't stop until he towered over her. His eyes snapped, his mouth flat with obvious displeasure. "Madam."

"Good morning, Pembroke," she greeted, wary. She'd been attempting to escape without his notice, without further opportunity for him to do as he'd threatened.

He sketched an abbreviated bow that seemed at odds with the tenseness hovering in the air between them. "Would you care to explain why I've been informed that you are traveling to London?"

Her hopes sagged. "I haven't the slightest notion why you were informed as I specifically directed the servants not to."

He looked arrogant and sinfully handsome at the same time. "Why would you keep it from me?"

Victoria aimed her gaze at a safer point over his shoulder. He was too gorgeous to look at, and doing so would only melt her determination all the more. She couldn't stop thinking about how that beautiful mouth had felt upon her most sensitive flesh, and no amount of perseverance and common sense appeared to lessen the effect he had on her.

She flushed. "I should think that's obvious."

He took her hands in his and she wished she'd worn gloves. She would have, but she'd thought she'd be alone and she couldn't abide by standing on ceremony when no one else was about to judge her. The contact sent her mind spinning.

"Are you running from me?"

"Of course not," she lied.

"Look at me." He caught her chin and forced her to meet his gaze. "I was right yesterday, though you attempted to brazen it out. You're afraid, aren't you?"

"Don't be preposterous," she snapped, irritated that he had chosen now of all times to become observant for the first time in their union. It was too late for him to be the husband she'd yearned for. Wasn't it? Yes, of course it was.

"I don't think I'm being preposterous," he said slowly, his fingers still lingering on her face. His eyes searched hers. He leaned into her, bending his head so that she was certain he would kiss her. "Not at all."

And then as if suddenly losing interest, he released her

and stepped away, leaving Victoria bereft and disappointed on the path. Had she imagined the heat in his gaze, the suggestion in his touch? The cool man before her seemed very much at odds with the passionate rake who had yanked up her skirts and pleasured her against the wall of the music room.

"I understand you have taken our gardens here under your care," he said, surprising her with his change of subject. "I must say, the transformations you've wrought are incredible."

She hadn't expected that he would care enough to ask the servants about her. She certainly hadn't expected that he would praise her efforts. Warmth unfurled within her belly, in spite of herself. "Thank you."

"I have it from the Head Gardener himself that you put an admirable amount of effort into restoring the grounds to their former splendor." His back was to her as he sniffed a luscious red bloom. "I expect the gardens hadn't been properly looked after since the times of the Tudors at least."

He turned to face her once more, a teasing grin on his lips, a rose in his hand. She wondered how he'd picked it without being pricked by a thorn. But then, he was Pembroke, beautiful and sleek and rife with charm. If anyone could fall into a rosebush without getting a single scratch, it would be him.

"Not the Tudors, I'm sure," she murmured, nervous to be at the center of his attention and compliments. Wasn't this precisely what she'd sought to avoid?

"Perhaps I exaggerate." He winked and closed the distance between them, holding the rose for her to smell.

She inhaled deeply of its glorious scent, never removing her gaze from his. "Roses possess the loveliest aroma, do you not think?"

"Not the loveliest." His expression sobered. "I prefer your scent."

Her heart took up a gallop. He had noticed her scent? Or was he merely continuing his aggressive campaign of wooing her? She decided to put him to the test. She was no longer as easily won as she once was. He'd seen to that himself.

"And what is my scent?"

"Orris root," he answered without hesitation. He dragged the silken petals of the rose down her bare throat. "I never realized before just how desirable I find it."

He'd known. She licked her suddenly dry lips. He was doing wicked things to her senses, making her want what she'd be better off not wanting. "Desirable?"

He nodded. "Almost as desirable as you."

His mouth brushed hers ever so softly, his lower lip slipping between hers. Just a whisper of touch, and yet it held so much fiery promise. This was different than the kisses they'd shared before. This kiss gave more than it took.

He caught her full upper lip between his teeth. She sighed and the kiss deepened, his tongue slipping inside to tease hers. He smelled like rich shaving soap. She locked her arms around his neck, leaning into his hard frame. It didn't seem fair that he could weaken her resolve with a few kind words and a kiss, but that didn't make it any less true.

Pembroke tore his lips from hers. "I don't want you to leave, Victoria," he murmured.

"I didn't want you to leave either," she reminded him, her voice breathless. "But you did."

"I'm here now." He gave her another slow, maddening kiss, his tongue dipping into her mouth and then retreating when she longed for more. "Come, let's go for a walk and enjoy the fruits of your labor."

She accepted the arm he proffered, and they began a leisurely stroll. It occurred to her that he was leading her farther away from the main house, out of sight of prying eyes. Pembroke hadn't walked with her like this since the days of their courtship, and it sent a wave of bittersweet nostalgia over her.

She cast him a sidelong glance. "I haven't been on a stroll about the gardens with a man in quite some time."

"I daresay." He cleared his throat, looking pensive. "I must thank you for the work you've done here in my absence, Victoria. I understand you've done a great deal more than just oversee the gardens. I'm afraid I've often been remiss in all my duties, not just one."

She had, and she was quite stunned he would even bother himself to find out what she'd done at Carrington House over the last few months. She nodded to stanch the flow of pleasure surging through her. He could tempt her with persuasive kisses and with flattery both, but five months of abandonment hardened a woman's resolve as few other things could.

"Thank you, my lord. My mother saw to it that I had a fair head for running a smooth household. Keeping ledgers has always been an odd hobby of mine anyway."

"Nevertheless, you needn't have. I didn't expect it of you."

His gratitude left her bemused. She'd expected to encounter the brazen seducer or the arrogant lord. But he was ever a man of many faces. She didn't know what to do with a Pembroke who wasn't disappearing and causing scandal. A Pembroke who was admiring and appreciative. A Pembroke who somehow wanted to win her back. Heavens, was that even possible? She couldn't think it. Wouldn't think it. The warmth of the sun had invaded her mind.

"I am your wife," she said simply. "It was my duty."

"Ah, but I did not do my duty to you."

She stopped and relinquished his arm, facing him again. Victoria had suffered far too much at his hands to pretend she hadn't. "No," she agreed quietly, "you did not."

His expression turned wry. "I have been thinking of how I can make amends."

"I suppose it wasn't entirely your fault," she said, taking pity on him a bit. "You didn't want a wife."

"It is true that my father forced my hand, but I begin to find I rather like having a wife." He caressed her cheek. "Don't go to London. Stay here with me. Carrington House

51

needs you."

Carrington House, he'd said, but not him. The omission was glaring. "I've drafted a list of changes that need to be made here. It's with the estate ledgers. You may feel free to use it."

"I don't want a list," he murmured, his tone low and intimate, sending warmth through her. "I want you. Tell me, what can be on this list of yours?"

She fought to keep her composure. "I recommend a raise for loyal retainers. It's difficult indeed to keep good servants these days."

He lowered his head, his lips exceedingly near to hers. "What else?"

She wanted him to kiss her but she forced herself to think. "The roof in the east wing has been leaking for some time. Funds need to be allocated for its repair, for if you don't act soon, I fear the roof will be in danger of collapse. I understand the east wing is the original manor house, dating back several centuries. It ought to be saved."

"Indeed?" His mouth remained distractingly close.

Her passion had become the historic, imposing, and awe-inspiring Carrington House. She'd made it her business to learn all of its shortcomings, all of its failures and weaknesses, all of its scars and wounds in need of mending. She was good at mending, figuratively speaking. In her family, she was the peacekeeper amongst her sisters.

"It is your family's history, my lord, not mine," she said, trying not to notice the proximity of his mouth to hers. "Were I you, I'd make more of an effort to preserve it. I realize there's an expense, but surely we can find the means."

"Surely."

"I do think you've stopped listening to me." She frowned.

"Of course I'm listening, darling. Do go on. What other ideas have you?" His tongue swept over her lower lip, tasting her as if she were a sugary treat. Something to be savored.

Dear heavens. Her mind went suddenly blank save for the need to feel his mouth upon hers.

"I can't recall," she admitted on a whisper.

"You see?" He grinned and gave her a quick kiss. "You must stay. What if I've questions about your list? What if you think of more changes to add to it? What if I want to ravish you again in the music room?"

His wicked question sent heat traveling through her, an answering pulse between her thighs. He was very good at destroying her defenses. Very good indeed. She hesitated, knowing that if she gave in to him it could well prove her undoing. But when she tried to muster the bitterness that had so long been her steadfast companion, she found it oddly absent.

I have been thinking of how I can make amends.

Could she trust him, this beautiful man before her who still remained so much a mystery? Dare she trust that he meant what he said? His words yesterday had revealed a part of her to herself that mystified and mortified her at the same time. She had remained at Carrington House not just out of duty but because it meant something to her. Because *he* meant something to her.

"I need you," he said finally. "Please stay."

Those three words tipped the scales inside her. "I shall stay," she relented. "For a few days."

"You won't regret it, my dear." He drew her hand to his lips for a lingering kiss, his stare searing her.

She fervently hoped he was right.

After turning about the gardens with Pembroke, Victoria returned to her rooms to announce her change of plans to her lady's maid, Keats, only to find that her husband had already called off her trip without her knowledge. He was very sure of her, she thought to herself. Perhaps too sure of her. It was a niggling concern in her mind as she joined him for dinner that evening as had become their routine.

"You are utterly beautiful," he murmured to her as he escorted her to dinner.

She'd chosen one of her best Worth gowns to wear that evening, a silk, satin, and velvet evening gown of dark green and ivory. The bodice hugged her curves and emphasized her bosom. It was complete with a skirt of shot cream silk and a drape of handmade French lace. The gown was from her trousseau, very different from the demure pastel gowns her mother had chosen for her before her marriage. Mother had never possessed an eye for fashion, and as a result, Victoria had faced her society debut with a wardrobe rife with ill-suiting frocks. She'd never had an occasion to wear a truly beautiful dress. Until now.

"You are very handsome yourself," she said, admiring the way his formal black trousers and coat hugged his impossibly tall and strong form.

He covered her hand with his for a moment and winked at her, the charming flirt once more. She supposed he was accustomed to hearing compliments from the fairer sex, but his words of praise were rare for her to hear, trapped away as she'd been in the country. Even before her marriage, however, she'd always considered herself plain. There were many women with far greater beauty than she possessed, women who commanded the interest of men like Pembroke. The thought curdled the warm glow of appreciation that had suffused her.

He seated her and lingered at her elbow, his spicy scent toying with her senses. He hadn't come to her chamber since the night he'd returned, and the knot of longing within her continued to grow, particularly after their tableau in the music room. She didn't want that knot. Indeed, she tried with all her might to undo it.

She treaded dangerous ground now. Victoria focused her gaze on the spray of English daisies and roses upon the table as she thanked Pembroke for his escort.

"You are most welcome," he said, his voice a low, velvety timbre in her ear.

Unless she was mistaken, he hesitated just long enough to deliver a quick nibble to her earlobe before straightening and rounding the table. His expression remained impassive as he sat. Had she imagined the delicious tug of his teeth upon her? The peculiar sensation of restlessness skittering through her suggested that she had not.

Awkward silence descended as the first course, a lovely smelling turtle soup, was laid before them. Pembroke abruptly directed the servants to leave them alone, startling her. She looked at him askance, trying not to notice how rakishly handsome he appeared with his too-long mahogany locks brushing the collar of his coat, his lively eyes sparkling in that too-handsome face, his mobile mouth always quirked with a hint of naughtiness.

"Everywhere I look, it seems I find another change wrought by the fair hand of my wife. You've done away with the powdered wigs," he noted when the door had closed, leaving them completely alone.

When she'd arrived at Carrington House, everything had been outmoded and dilapidated. She knew from experience that these days, country houses rarely required footmen to wear the wigs so preferred by previous generations unless it was the most formal of occasions. She was once again at a loss. He had always seemed far too busy being a devil-may-care to pay attention to the dress of his servants.

"Almost no one requires it any longer," she offered. "Scratchy, dreadfully uncomfortable things, I'm told, though still preferable to powder."

"Indeed?" He raised a brow. "Do you make it a habit of inquiring after the welfare of all our footmen?"

"Most certainly not." She flushed, having difficulty concentrating with his gaze pinned upon her. "I asked my lady's maid when I contemplated the change. It seemed so silly to continue the practice unless we actually had guests in residence. Do you object, my lord?"

"Pray call me Will, my dear. We are on decidedly intimate terms now, are we not? As it happens, I don't mind the absence of the wigs. Always looked as if they were about to slide off anyhow." He tasted his soup. "Delightful. I shall have to pass my compliments to Mrs. Rufton."

She hadn't known much of Pembroke as the master of his estate. But from what she'd gleaned from belowstairs gossip related to her by her lady's maid, he hadn't been the sort to notice anything in his household unless it affected his own pleasures. Yet it appeared he had gone to great length to take note of even the tiniest changes she'd made.

She wasn't certain if it was because he'd taken an interest in her, or if it was because he disliked her taking up the reins. "I waited quite some time to begin making my mark here at Carrington House," she offered, feeling as if she ought to explain. "You never answered my correspondence, and so I suppose I took your silence as acceptance."

"Of course you would." He flashed her a smile that she couldn't quite decipher. "May I ask you something, my dear?"

"You may." She stilled in the act of sampling Mrs. Rufton's rich soup. "But I cannot promise an answer."

His smile deepened, and it served to only enhance the startling effect of his good looks. "Everyone, from the new housekeeper to Mrs. Rufton to the very proper Wilton, has been raving about how wonderful a mistress you are. I can see much has changed, and yet when I arrived, there was an inordinate amount of dust in my chamber. Why?"

She felt her cheeks go warm. Oh dear. It seemed her husband's newfound skills of observation extended to all matters. She was embarrassed that he'd caught her childish act of defiance. "You were not mistaken." She paused. "I directed Mrs. Morton to tell the housemaids not to touch your chamber."

"Indeed?"

"I had no reason to think you'd be returning any time soon," she added hastily. "But I must admit that I was also hoping that should you return you'd suffer a very unpleasant welcome."

He laughed at her admission. At least, she reasoned, he wasn't angry with her for allowing the dust to grow in his chamber. Lord knew it had given her endless amounts of satisfaction to imagine him sneezing away in it during the months of his absence.

"I daresay you won that battle, my dear. I'm sure I was sneezing my wits out all evening when I first arrived."

She shared his smile, aware she was ever falling more under his potent spell. "You deserved it, my lord."

"Will," he reminded her.

"Will," she said, trying his Christian name on her tongue. Will seemed fitting. Pembroke had been the rogue husband who'd abandoned her. It was as if Will was the charming, perceptive man who'd taken his place. Except Will and Pembroke were one and the same, knave and charmer in one gloriously handsome form. There was the rub.

His expression sobered. "I confess I do like hearing my name on your lovely lips."

She forced herself to recall the awful months he'd left her to cavort with other women in London, lest she throw herself at him there in the dining room. "You deserved it, Will," she said pointedly before returning her attention to her soup.

"Touché." He raised his wine goblet to her in mock salute. "But I still enjoy hearing you say my name."

She looked back up at him. "I'm sure you've grown accustomed to hearing it on the lips of many other *ladies*." The emphasis she put upon the word left no doubt that she did not think any of them had been ladies at all.

"Am I to be forever reminded of my past misdeeds?"

"I'm not one to quibble over definitions, but I do seem to recall that only a fortnight ago, you were engaging in misdeeds at the Belgravia house with a Signora Rosignoli. That hardly seems so far away as to be deemed past." It was her turn to raise a brow. "Until you've proven you've changed for good, I remind myself as much as I remind you." For her own self-preservation, she added silently.

"I've told you before that I never wanted to hurt you, Victoria." He put down his spoon. "My battle is with my father, not you, and I regret that you were caught up in the crossfire."

The acknowledgment seemed genuine, but so had his interest in her during their courtship. Even if he was being honest now, she didn't know if it was enough. "Thank you," she offered simply. "I am gratified you've realized that much, at least."

"You are most welcome." He studied her intently. "Now, I find I've tired of the soup course. Have you?"

Her turtle soup had long gone cold. She nodded, watching warily as he rose from the table and stalked toward her. He stopped when he was at her side, leaning his hip negligently against the table. He framed her face with his large hands.

"We both know I never wanted to be a husband when I married you," he said at last, his tone grave.

His acknowledgment had an air of deep candor to it, far more than his effortless flirtation and charming grins did. She searched his bright gaze, wondering if she could trust him. Wondering if she should. It occurred to her that what had happened in the past did not hold as much power over her life as what could happen in the future.

"And what of now?" she asked. "What do you want now?" It was the question that seemed to matter the most.

His gaze grew shuttered. "I have a duty to do by you."

She frowned, trying to understand him. His hands were still a warm, tempting touch on her face. "Duty is not a want."

"Sometimes it becomes a want," he murmured, lowering his mouth to crush hers.

The hunger of his kiss took her completely by surprise. He slid his palms down over her arms and hauled her to her feet. Her chair toppled over behind her. She clutched at his shoulders, opening to his questing tongue. His words swirled through her mind, confusing her all the more. Was he saying he wanted her? Or that he still considered her a duty?

She couldn't be sure, but all she did know for certain was that he was undoing the hidden jet buttons at the back of her bodice. He dragged the lace-capped sleeves down over her arms, drawing her gown, chemise, and corset cover to her waist. The creamy tops of her breasts were exposed above her satin corset.

He tore his mouth from hers to gaze upon the flesh he'd revealed. His eyes were hot, glittering with lust and, unless she was mistaken, appreciation.

"Scarlet?"

Flushing again, she looked at the extravagant red corset she'd had commissioned in Paris before her nuptials. "It's my favorite color," she said, slightly embarrassed by her whim.

"I adore it." He dropped a kiss upon each of her breasts, cupping them through the fabric and stiff whalebone that helped her curves to attain the proper shape. "I'd adore it even more if it was on the floor."

She gasped, reality returning to her at his bold pronouncement. "We mustn't. Not during dinner. What would the servants say?"

He looked up at her, a wicked expression on his face. "I expect they'd say that I've gone mad, and I'm afraid they wouldn't be too far off the mark."

"I must say I prefer mad Will over sane Pembroke any day," she confessed.

The old Pembroke certainly wouldn't have all but made love to her over dinner. Goodness, what was she thinking, allowing him to cajole her into such scandalous behavior? Bad enough he had her at sixes and sevens. Now, she was *en dishabille* during the soup course.

"I suppose you're right." He sighed and began straightening her desperately askew bodice. "It wouldn't do to ruin the servants' proper opinion of us. But I'm afraid I cannot wait much longer for you, my dear, else I'll go mad in truth."

He wanted her.

He wanted the shy woman he'd married for money. His attentions had not been feigned. His scorching passion in the music room had been real. Her stomach upended like a tipped teacup. Oh dear. She hadn't permitted herself to even think of sharing the marriage bed with him again. It was far too tempting, far too dangerous to her heart. But part of her didn't care. Part of her longed for passion. For *him*.

His hands were gentle as they righted her gown over her bared shoulders before reaching round the back to redo the hidden procession of buttons. "May I come to you tonight?"

The request sent her heart into a wild rhythm as passion slid through her body like warm honey. She closed her eyes for a moment, uncertain of what her answer should be. Very probably, it ought to be an outright "no". And yet, she couldn't deny she was drawn to him as ever. What could be the harm? It was only her heart at stake.

"Yes," she whispered. "You may."

chapter five

H E'D WON. ALREADY.
     Will lingered in his study long after dinner's
     end, nursing a brandy and soda water,
brooding. He'd finally gotten what he wanted. His cock had
been hard as hell for the duration of dinner, but he'd wanted
to give Victoria time to prepare herself for his visit, so he'd
gone off to his study.

The trouble was, once alone, his conscience had set in,
the very conscience he'd no longer thought he possessed.
He cursed and tossed back a bit more of his drink, disgusted
with himself. Returning to the country had turned him
maudlin. Somehow, over the course of the time he'd been
at Carrington House, he'd grown to like his wife. He
admired her for her skills at running his household and for
her strong will. Back in London, he hadn't considered the
particular conundrum in which he now found himself so
precariously mired.

He was poised on the precipice of success. In less than
a sennight, he had wooed his wife into accepting him in her
bed again. He should be thrilled. Christ, he should be

61

stripping her out of her naughty French undergarments and sliding inside her sweet little cunny right now. He shouldn't be hiding away in his study.

With his ultimate goal so close at hand, he wasn't supposed to be feeling empathy toward his wife. She was a means to an end, a necessary duty. He definitely wasn't supposed to be so achingly attracted to her. Bloody hell, feeling anything at all most certainly was not part of his plan.

Yet, he did.

Yes, he liked her. He liked her sharp mind and the way she pursed her lips when she was mulling over something and the way she held herself with quiet grace when she entered a room. He liked her snapping eyes and her long, luscious blonde hair, and good Lord he positively loved helping to unleash the wicked streak within her.

This was a strange development indeed. Of all the women he'd flirted with and bedded in his life, and it was an admittedly lengthy list, he could honestly say he hadn't truly admired many of them. Perhaps he hadn't even admired *any* of them, now that he thought on it.

A conundrum indeed, one of the worst sort. Victoria was waiting for him in her chamber, willing and ready. And yet here he lingered in his study with a tumbler of spirits, realizing he harbored an alarming depth of sentiment for his wife, the very woman who had been foisted upon him, the woman he'd spent months resenting, the woman he'd thought he could so easily forget. But he wouldn't forget. Not now. Not her.

He tossed back the remainder of his brandy and soda water. It was foolish to linger any longer like a callow virgin on his wedding night. He was no callow virgin, and he'd already had his wedding night. Even so, he had a bothersome feeling that what awaited him would leave him forever changed.

Victoria had dismissed Keats. She wore only a silk wrapper and a few dabs of orris root at her throat and wrists. Will had told her he preferred the scent.

Will.

Her husband.

It seemed so odd, so improbable, that the man whose presence she eagerly awaited was the same man who had wed and abandoned her, the same man she'd sworn she'd never forgive. Her mind told her she was a candidate for the lunatic asylum. Had she learned nothing from the five months of loneliness and swirling scandal she'd had to face alone? Perhaps not, for all she could think of now was the devastating way he'd looked at her for the duration of dinner. Like he wanted to devour her.

He had kissed her as if he were a starving man and she the feast before him. He touched her and set her aflame. She wanted him very much, wanted more of what had happened in the music room. At that thought, a solid series of knocks sounded on the door joining their chambers together.

Despite knowing he would be coming to her, she started, a bout of nerves gripping her. She tightened the belt at her waist and consulted her reflection in the looking glass. Her hair was down, a curling sweep of locks to her waist. The lamp light was low, bathing the chamber in a warm glow.

Another knock interrupted her worried contemplation. Her mouth went dry.

She took a deep breath. "Enter."

The door creaked open and she thought she must have one of the footmen oil it. Then her husband filled the doorway and she quite forgot everything. He wore a black dressing gown, his large feet and strong, masculine calves peeking beneath its hem. Her face went warm and she was sure she was flushed as a ripe apple. Her eyes traveled up from the tie drawn at his lean waist to the sliver of his bare chest visible. Their gazes clashed as a delicious tide of longing washed over her.

"Victoria," he murmured. "I was afraid you'd have fallen asleep."

She swallowed, opting for levity. "Of course I couldn't sleep for fear of another midnight invasion that required the aid of Mr. Dickens."

He winced. "My nose is still tender to the touch."

"You didn't even bear a mark," she returned, not believing a bit of it.

"Spoken with nary a trace of regret." He tapped the facial feature in question. "Truly, it will never again be the same."

"A lifelong reminder never to sneak into my bedchamber uninvited." She kept her tone tart. Oh, what was she doing, trading barbs with the man who had caused her such heartache these many months? She tried to cling to the endless list of ladies who'd been connected to his name in scandal, but they'd begun to fall away like the petals of a rose the first time he'd looked at her and truly seen her as a woman.

Perhaps she had revealed the wayward path of her thoughts, for his expression shifted, his jawline hardening. "Are you certain you're ready for me tonight? I will wait, Victoria."

No.

But she couldn't tell him as much. Wouldn't tell him as much, for she didn't want to let him think he possessed that much power over her emotions. "I'm ready. Please, come in." She could do her duty—for that was what this truly was, after all. She mustn't allow herself to think otherwise. Tonight was duty and pleasure bound into one.

He'd been lingering at the threshold but at her urging, he finally crossed the invisible boundary between his chamber and hers. The adjoining door squeaked closed again at his back. He was unbearably handsome. His thick hair was ruffled, as if he'd been passing a hand through it. Had he been as nervous as she?

They both began moving toward each other, meeting in

the center of the room. She gazed up at him, framing his beautiful face with her palms. His cheeks were slightly scratchy with the texture of the whiskers he'd shaved that morning. She rather enjoyed the prickle against her skin.

She searched his eyes but found them unreadable. "This isn't a lark for you, is it?" Somehow, there was an important distinction.

His expression tightened, his smile fading. "It isn't a lark. I want you." He guided her hand down over the silky robe to the rigid outline of his manhood, pressing himself into her. "There's no feigning my reaction to you."

"Good heavens." She touched him, hard and heavy, as an answering blossom of heat opened deep within her.

He slid his arms round her waist and drew her more firmly against his body. "It's been far too long since I've made love to you, wife."

Victoria lost the ability to speak. Without the proper layers of clothing, boning, and petticoats between them, she could feel the strength and maleness of him in a way she never had before. His body molded to hers was a new and enticing experience that sent an exquisite ache to her core.

She liked it.

He lowered his mouth to hers, giving her a possessive kiss. She opened, playing her tongue against his. He tasted of spirits. Her hands settled on his shoulders, soaking in his potency. A spurt of restlessness kicked up within her stomach, longing settling lower along with a languorous throbbing.

The kiss deepened. He cupped her bottom through her thin wrapper, ensuring their bodies touched in all the right places.

"Finally," he muttered, tearing his lips from hers. "I don't have to wrestle with hectares of fabric."

She laughed despite the heady mix of sensations setting her at sixes and sevens. "A gown with a train is in fashion."

"To hell with fashion. Have you any idea how many silly trains I've trampled at balls?" He caught the ends of the tie at her waist and pulled. Her wrapper gaped, revealing nearly all of her breasts. One more tug and the ends completely fell apart. He ran hot palms over her shoulders, shucking the garment from her body entirely. "I prefer you naked."

And naked she was. Victoria fought the urge to cover herself. She stood very still, watching from beneath lowered lashes as her husband's warm gaze ran over her body. She waited, knowing she was no beauty, that she was in fact rather small and spindly without all her trappings. Keats was very adept at showing her to advantage, but now she had no such assistance. She was sure he must have seen lovelier women, perhaps even his Italian opera singer. The thought made her stiffen.

"Why the ferocious frown, my dear?" He traced her lips with a light touch, running his finger down her neck to her breasts. He circled her nipple in a lazy path that had the bud tightening and her body aching for more. "You are more beautiful than I recalled."

He thought her beautiful? Her gaze snapped to his face, searching his expression for the slightest hint of insincerity. There was none. His eyes were direct, his expression frank and admiring. No man had ever paid her a compliment as kind in her life. True, there had been her fair share of effusive flattery by gentleman who looked at her and saw her father's fat purse and not her true self. But this was somehow different. Was it the way he'd said it, or simply that he *had* said it, that mattered so much?

A sudden surge of courage overtook her. She wanted to see him as well. She made short work of the knot at his waist. His dressing gown slid to the floor in a soft whisper of sound. He was breathtaking. The knot of desire building within her grew. He was lean yet muscled, his chest broad and defined. But what truly attracted her attention was not his taut stomach or the long, strong lines of his legs. No indeed, it was the rigid arousal jutting proudly from the apex of his thighs.

Good heavens. She nearly swallowed her tongue. She

certainly hadn't seen *that* on their wedding night. Blushing furiously, she forced her gaze back up to his face. The grin on his sensual mouth was positively wicked. Perhaps she'd wandered into water that was well over her head. She felt very much as if she were drowning.

It seemed he sensed her sudden worry. He tipped her chin up. "Don't fret, my dear. We shall go as slowly as you like."

It wasn't precisely the speed of their joining that concerned her, but rather the mechanics of it. Now she well understood the stab of pain she'd felt the last time. Would it hurt again?

"You're worrying your lip." He cupped her face in his large, capable hands and delivered a tender kiss to the lip in question. "You mustn't think too much. Only feel."

"Feeling is what lands me in trouble," she couldn't resist pointing out. She certainly felt too much for the debonair man standing nude before her.

He grinned down at her. "What is life without a spot of trouble now and again?"

Easy, she supposed, for him to say. He'd never had to move an ocean away from the world he knew only to be abandoned in a countryside with naught but a gaggle of servants for company. But holding on to resentment couldn't be beneficial to the tentative truce she'd struck with her husband, and she knew it. Perhaps he was right after all. Maybe she should trust him.

Could she? Though it was balmy in her chamber from the warmth of the summer sun, she shivered.

"Cold?" He scooped her up into his arms in one effortless motion. "I can warm you."

No one had ever carried her before either. Apparently, it was to be a night of many firsts. Victoria threw her arms about his neck to hold on to him as he crossed the chamber to her bed. She took the opportunity to study his handsome profile. His jaw was strong, stippled with the day's growth of dark whiskers. Unlike many English gentlemen, he eschewed a beard and mustache. She found it enhanced the physical beauty of his face. Mesmerized, she lifted a hand to again feel the rough texture of his stubble against her palm. He turned slightly to press a kiss to her inner wrist. A jolt of pleasure shot through her. *You mustn't think too much*, he had said. *Only feel.*

How freeing it would be to do so with him. To trust if she dared.

He laid her gently upon the bed before joining her, his long form stretched out alongside hers. Their bodies were intimately pressed together for their entire lengths. She was so petite that her feet only reached his calves. His arousal jutted against the nip of her waist. Victoria kept her gaze locked on his, almost afraid that if she looked away, she would become lost in the stormy seas of emotion attempting to carry her off.

He slid a possessive arm around her, anchoring her to him even more firmly. "I want you." His mouth was close to hers, his breath warm and intoxicating. The low growl of his deep voice went directly to her core.

With a moan, she ended the distance between them by kissing him. She opened to his questing tongue, tasting him, wanting to devour him the way his kisses threatened to consume her. She threaded her arms around his neck, fingers sinking into his dark hair. He invaded her senses. She tasted him, smelled his scent, so deliciously male and his.

He threw a lean leg over her, pinning her to the bed. She was at his mercy now, and it sent a decadent sluice of desire over her suddenly heated skin. Every bit of her had come to life. Her nipples ached for his mouth and touch, her core for his driving possession inside her. If he wanted her, she wanted him more, with an intensity that drove her near to madness.

Their kisses ended. Will dragged his mouth down her throat. She tilted her head back against the pillow to allow him better access. The hot, moist pressure of his lips upon her sensitized skin was enough to have her squirming for more. He groaned as if he too felt the same undeniable pull, its wild thrill, sense of overwhelming pleasure. He kissed his way to her breasts, cupping the tingling mounds in his large hands before lowering his head to suck a throbbing nipple.

Victoria arched into him, incapable of stopping the moan that fled her lips. He tortured her flesh, alternately sucking and rolling his tongue over and around the engorged bud. While he plied an equal seduction on the other breast, his fingers skipped down over her belly and dipped into the wet slit of her sex. He teased the oversensitive nub hidden within her folds, and she jerked into his knowing hand. He continued on, sucking and rubbing her, sucking and rubbing, until her body was working against him in a primitive rhythm.

Her breath tore from her in fast gasps, mewling cries of passion caught in her throat. Surely, she managed to think through the murk of her wanton mind, this was heaven on earth. Nothing could ever again feel so incredible. She felt as if she were about to burst.

And then she did, shaking against him, her eyes closed tightly to savor the amazing sensations rocketing through her. There were no words for it, save—

"Pure bliss," she murmured, aware that he'd addled her so much with his lovemaking that she was becoming nonsensical, speaking her private thoughts aloud.

"I agree." Her husband kissed the inner curve of her breast, then raked his teeth delicately over her nipple once more. His finger traveled lower, sinking inside her.

Her breath escaped from her lungs. She wanted—no needed—to feel him inside her. She ached with wanting more. In and out, his finger pushed, delving inside her so deeply that she feared she'd burst again.

"Are you ready for me?"

She nodded, eyes still closed.

"Look at me, Victoria."

Startled by his use of her name, she obeyed, blinking to find his handsome face still perilously near to her bare breasts. Her nipples were pink, glistening with the wetness of his kiss. She glanced lower, to where his hand pressed between her thighs. Embarrassment hit her. Her skirts had obscured her view of him pleasuring her in the music room. This was different. All too wanton. She turned her head away, staring instead at the drawn drapes over her window.

It was the window where she'd held a constant vigil in the early days of her abandonment, hoping to see him return. She'd never told anyone, not even Maggie in one of the many rambling letters she'd sent, bemoaning her loneliness.

Suddenly, it all seemed too much, the mingle of pleasure he'd given her with the awful hurt. She stiffened, uncertainty reeling her in. But the passion remained, soothing her traitorous body into wanting him, regardless of the past. Confusing her.

"Don't pull away from me." His tone was firm, allowing no opposition. "Let me bring you pleasure. Let me make you spend."

It didn't escape her notice that he spoke of pleasure and not of love. Had she expected him to fall at her feet like a lovelorn suitor? The same man who had coldly told her he had no need or want of a wife? Perhaps her heart was too fragile to allow him this breathtaking intimacy.

He nudged her legs apart and came over her completely, his manhood resting heavily against her, his knees at either side of her hips. She didn't want to see him, for if she did, she would give in. She laid very still, eyes fixed on the drapes.

"Look at me," he insisted again. "Damn it, Victoria. I'll not force my own wife."

It wouldn't require force, and she knew it. There was a note of frustration in his voice, perhaps even hurt. He didn't understand her, it seemed, any more than she understood him. Or herself, for that matter. Her resolve wavered. His body was a welcome weight upon hers, and she wanted him to finish what they'd begun. She turned back to him, afraid that she truly did love him after all.

It was a crippling realization.

His stare skewered her, hot and laden with possibilities. "Do you want me or not, sweet?" As he posed the question, he once again teased her pearl, applying just the right amount of pressure to send more pleasure washing over her.

"If you swear to stay," she blurted. She was very much aware that asking something so monumental of him at a time such as this was unfair. She also knew that, by law, she had absolutely no right to make any demands upon him whatsoever, wife or no. Even if he agreed now, he could rescind his promise later should it suit him. She was allowing him to see past her brazen façade, and she wasn't sure she ought to.

He stilled, stopping the ministrations that made her wild. "Pardon?"

Had he not heard her or did he simply want to humiliate her by requiring her to repeat her request? She faltered, caught in his gaze, not knowing what to do. Finally, she decided to stay the course. "Will you stay here with me? And if you must leave, will you take me with you?"

Will stared, his expression as impenetrable as his eyes. "Is that what you want of me?"

His hand was still between her thighs. Her heart beat fast. "Of course." It was, wasn't it? Yes, it had to be. The last few days had done much damage to her defenses, and she didn't think she could survive yet another abandonment unscathed. She could control so many things in her life, but not truly the things she most wanted to manage. She could not help her feelings for him. Burying them, holding on to her anger, had not changed them. He had stripped her bare this night, and she'd never been more vulnerable.

"I shall do my best by you," he said, a note of almost harsh honesty entering his tone. "I vow it."

You mustn't think too much. Only feel.

She wasn't certain she could. Her mind spun faster than the wheels on a runaway carriage. He hadn't given her the promise she wanted. What in heaven's name was his best? Dare she trust him enough to discover?

"I shall try not to hurt you again, Victoria," he added, his voice softening. "If I leave, you are welcome to accompany me."

She supposed it had to be concession enough, particularly coming from him. He hovered over her, so very large and beautiful. The time for speaking was over. Victoria reached out to him, pulling him more fully atop her.

He came down over her, his mouth crushing hers in another kiss. Her breasts were pressed firmly against him. His manhood was stiff and thick, prodding her. He toyed with her sex, rubbing his cock against the slick flesh, flicking over the tender nub hidden there.

She opened her legs, allowing him to guide her so that she wrapped her legs round his waist. Then he pressed his arousal against her. Instinctively, she jerked up and into him, wanting to feel him inside her. He entered her slowly at first, just the tip dipping into her. No pain this time. Only pleasure. A searing, bone-deep pleasure.

She moaned against his lips, gripping his broad shoulders in an effort to pull him even closer. Somehow, she couldn't have enough of him.

He stopped at her moan, breaking the kiss to glance down at her, their noses nearly brushing against each other. "Are you sure, darling?"

Victoria nodded, incapable of coherent speech, and slid her palms down over his strong back to his buttocks. She urged him to come inside her more fully, drawing him into her. He obeyed her unspoken plea, pushing deeper. If she had thought his touch had driven her mad, it was nothing compared to the onslaught of sensation she felt now.

He began a wicked rhythm, and she matched him, raising her hips eagerly for more. Each thrust built the intensity of her pleasure, bringing her closer and closer to the point of fulfillment once again. He groaned, increasing his speed as he pumped into her before lowering his head to claim her lips in another kiss. His tongue swept into her mouth, possessive and demanding. When he reached between their bodies, she couldn't stave off the ripples of bliss that began to overtake her. She shuddered, coming helplessly undone, crying out her pleasure.

Her climax seemed to drive him wild, for he propelled himself into her even faster, harder and deeper. He tore his mouth from hers to throw his head back, eyes closed. The expression on his face was one of pure ecstasy. She'd never seen him look so unguarded before, and watching him as he took his pleasure filled her with a new feeling of warmth for him.

In another series of thrusts, he stiffened against her, a groan so low it almost sounded like a growl coming from his throat. She knew another wave of heady passion as the wet spurt of his seed went inside her. And then he collapsed atop her completely, breathing heavily. He pressed a reverent kiss to the side of her neck.

In the aftermath of their desire, neither one of them spoke. Victoria gently brushed a lock of hair from his forehead and held him, a quiet sense of happiness taking root within her.

chapter six

WILL WOKE TO THE STRANGE PRESENCE OF HIS wife in his bed. He blinked his eyes open as a thin sliver of sunlight cut through the drapery of the windows. She was curled against his side as if she were a little cat. A handful of long blonde curls tickled his nose as he assessed the tableau before him.

Devil take it. He was actually in his wife's chamber. He hadn't returned to his. He had never, not once in his life, slept for the entire night with a woman. What the hell was the matter with him? One week in the country and he was noticing things like dust, housekeepers and footmen, and allowing the wife he hadn't wanted to drape herself all over him and choke him with her wild hair. His right arm was even wrapped around her, anchoring her to his side as if it were where she belonged.

Christ.

Careful not to wake Victoria, he rescued his arm and raised a hand to pluck her curls from his face. They smelled like her sweet perfume. Damn if his cock didn't harden at the scent. He wanted her again. With a muttered curse, he dropped her curls as though they were made of asps.

He had to escape her clutches, perhaps go for a head-clearing ride. He gently laid back his portion of the bedclothes and sat up. Then he made the mistake of glancing in his wife's direction. She was still gloriously nude, lying on her side with her back to him. The position and the peeled-back coverlets provided him with a fair view of her pale, perfectly rounded backside. Even her back, small and curved into a dip at her narrow waist, appealed to him. Her hair was a riot of golden tresses tangled across both his pillow and hers.

His pillow?

True, he supposed everything in the house was his, whether or not it had received an improvement from the marriage settlement. But he certainly didn't want to get in the habit of thinking he belonged in her bedchamber unless it was for the sort of passion they'd shared the previous evening. After which he would bloody well leave.

A slow, steady ache took up fastidious residence in his skull. What had he been thinking to allow her to cozen him into making promises to her? By God, he had never made a promise to any woman.

An odd feeling lodged in his chest. Guilt. His wife was turning him into a saint. He wouldn't have this. Not a bit of it. But her sweet bottom was certainly a tempting sight. His cock pointedly reminded him of that fact yet again. What was the harm in indulging in another bout of lovemaking? He longed to lose himself inside her wetness, fill her with his seed. Get her heavy with his child.

Sweet Jesus, his depravity truly knew no bounds, for the thought of her carrying his child made him even harder. This was not the proper order of things. Something was decidedly wrong with him. Making love to her wasn't just a task he had taken on in the name of restoring his funds any longer. He'd lost sight of duty and necessity. It wasn't even a game, a sharp blade to slice the ennui. It was sheer madness.

He leaned down, unable to stop himself from the folly, and kissed the arch of her bare shoulder. He flicked his tongue against her skin, tantalized by the smooth creaminess of her, the taste of sweetness mingled with a hint of salt. She made a breathy sound and rolled over onto her back. Not enough of the coverlet traveled with her, leaving one of her generous breasts peeking out at him. Her pink nipple pointed up, hard and ready for his mouth. He wanted to suck it until she bucked wildly against him as she had last night.

He gave in to temptation and cupped her breast in his palm, loving the way her nipple puckered and tightened against him. She truly was a gem. Perhaps there was something to be said after all for American ladies who wore seductive silks and walloped their husbands in the nose with fine English literature.

Will kissed her then before he lost complete control of his upper works. She was slow to wake, but after a bit of coaxing, she parted her lips and sighed into his mouth. Kissing her was a prelude to something he wanted much more than mere kissing. Unable to help himself, he pushed the obstruction of her coverlet away so that he could straddle her naked body. He needed to be inside her. His hands were on both her breasts, her fingers tangled in his hair, her petite limbs wrapped round his waist.

Ah, hell. If this was what living with his wife was like, he'd never leave. It seemed there were benefits to waking up in her bed. He skimmed his fingers down between their bodies to the juncture of her thighs and the prize he sought. Her cunny was already slick and ready for him. He flicked his thumb over the sensitive nub just the way he'd discovered she liked. Her body was incredibly responsive, jerking against him.

If he didn't take her soon, he'd explode. He positioned himself at her entrance, raining kisses down over her throat, and thrust. All lucid thought fled his mind. His entire world became focused on losing himself in his wife's luscious body. In and out he stroked, loving the throaty moans he produced from her lovely lips. He pumped at a fast pace, knowing from the heaviness of her breathing that she preferred her lovemaking to be deep and intense just the way he did.

Caught in the throes of heady desire, he almost didn't hear her half sigh, half-whispered words.

"I love you."

She loved him? Had he heard her aright? He couldn't have, and she was still dazed with sleep. Surely she didn't love him. Still, somehow her declaration had the opposite effect on him than it should have, because he was suddenly about to climax. Instantly. He couldn't hold it in any longer. Throwing his head back like a conquering warrior, he spilled his seed inside her.

When he was finally spent, he rolled to the side and forced himself to get out of her bed before he decided to live there forever. Empathy was one thing, guilt another. But this inexplicable, unavoidable attraction he felt for her was becoming altogether unacceptable. He couldn't allow it to rule his life. He had to remember that his primary focus was saving himself from financial ruin and not playing lovelorn suitor to his wife. The very wife the duke had chosen for him

"Will?"

Her sleepy voice called after him, her tone questioning. He hadn't even looked at her in the aftermath of their lovemaking. He was afraid to, by God. He stalked across the chamber and recovered his discarded dressing gown. Perhaps he owed her an explanation for his boorish behavior this morning, but he had none. He was more bollixed up than he'd ever been in his admittedly bollixed life.

"Will?"

Christ. Her voice sounded unsteady. He turned to look at her as he stuffed his arms into his sleeves and knotted the belt at his waist. She had covered her beautiful body and appeared incredibly small in the large high tester. Her hair was still a halo of riotous curls around her face. She had told him she loved him, and he had embarrassed himself in response by coming as quickly as a lad having his first maid.

He wasn't meant to love her, nor she him.

Love didn't exist for anyone other than silly chits and proud mamas.

Victoria was waiting for him to respond. He cleared his throat. "Good morning, my dear." And with nothing more, he turned on his heel and took his leave from her chamber before he did something even more imprudent like run back to join his delightfully rumpled wife in bed.

Had she told him she loved him? After the door joining her husband's chamber to hers snapped closed, Victoria sank back into her pillows, mortified. She'd been convinced she was in the midst of a wonderful dream, overtaken by the sensations he evoked in her. It had been a sinfully lovely way to wake up, to her husband's impassioned kisses and caresses. She hadn't meant to say those three words aloud.

She could pretend she'd never spoken them, carry on as Will had, as if he'd never heard her. But she wasn't naïve, and she knew he'd heard her all too well. It was why he'd run off at the first opportunity.

His reaction to her blunder was crushing. She'd told him she loved him, and he'd offered her nothing more than a cool "good morning" before disappearing. Perhaps she had made a grave mistake in allowing him into her bed, for in so doing she had also allowed him back into her heart. If indeed he'd ever left it.

Her bed still smelled like him. Reluctantly, she rose and sought out her wrapper, still pooled on the thick carpet. Odd, but she felt more alone now than she had in all the months he'd been gone.

With a sigh, she headed to the bell pull and rang for

Keats. Although she'd like nothing better than to hide from Will for the remainder of the day, she knew doing so would merely be a childish postponement of the inevitable reckoning. She crossed the room as she waited, pulling the drapes aside to stare down into the slightly gloomy sunshine of the day.

If only he'd said something more than "good morning".

Will was still cursing himself for being an ass by the time his wife glided into the morning room for their customary shared breakfast. He could have managed a bit more than a polite greeting earlier, and he knew it. He paused at her entrance, in the act of helping himself to the kippers, bacon, eggs, and toast on the sideboard.

She wore a vibrant morning gown of deep indigo with French lace peeking from a high décolletage and an embroidered skirt that was cut away to reveal more lace beneath. Although her attire was quite modest, he could envision the delectable curves and breasts beneath her fashionable wasp waist and billowing silk. When last he'd seen her, she'd been nude and he'd just been inside her.

He swallowed hard, willing his instant arousal to subside.

"Good morning," he offered through suddenly stiff lips. Christ, she was turning him into a halfwit. Here he was, tossing her the same meaningless pleasantries that had already put an invisible rift between them. He could sense her withdrawal from him just as surely as he could smell the crisp aroma of the bacon before him.

As if to prove his point, she cast him a look that was positively frigid. Her diminutive features were immobile in her ordinarily expressive face. Rather than meeting his gaze, her eyes were trained upon something on the far wall of the breakfast room. An old family portrait, perhaps, the one of the fourth duke posed with a favorite hunting dog. Anything but him.

He'd hurt her, he realized, and just when he'd promised not to. He winced, watching as she allowed the butler to seat her in an equally icy silence. Though she did thank poor Wilton with a forced smile.

Time for him to pay the forfeit, he decided. He finished adding a heap of eggs to his plate. "May I put together a plate for you, my dear?"

She still refused to look directly at him, but she did deign to give him a regal nod. "You may."

The ever-efficient Wilton appeared at his elbow, kind enough to take Will's plate back to the table for him so that he could dedicate his attention to his wife's. He selected an array of meats, toast and jam. He'd noticed that she never touched her eggs, but she had a fondness for marmalade.

He placed her plate before her with a flourish. "Your breakfast, my lady."

He was near enough to her to catch a whiff of her sweet perfume. Her golden locks had been twisted into an artful coiffure by her lady's maid, the tresses so shiny they glinted. She refused to turn toward him, leaving him only with her profile. A lone sapphire earring dangled against her creamy neck. Damn if he wasn't jealous of the bauble for its proximity to her soft skin.

"Thank you, Pembroke." Her voice possessed an underlying note of emotion. "Please do enjoy yours."

He'd been dismissed.

It occurred to him that he was lingering like a lovesick swain at her side. What the hell was he doing, staring at the pretty shell of his wife's ear, thinking about kissing her neck before the butler? He was a candidate for the lunatic asylum. His fall from grace was complete.

Feeling even more like an imbecile, he seated himself. How could she rattle him so, this tiny scrap of a woman he'd never even given half a thought to until last week? It was ridiculous. Embarrassing. Absurd.

"Did you say something, my lord?"

He paused, forkful of eggs poised in *medias res* to his

mouth. Dear God. Had he been muttering aloud to himself? He tamped down his self-loathing, flashing her a patient smile. "Nothing at all."

They were quiet for a time then, but for the tinny sound of cutlery on fine china. He was grateful for the respite. Old Mrs. Rufton still excelled at cooking, and he savored every bite of her moist, fresh-herb-laden eggs. Not to mention the divine taste of the bacon on his tongue. Perhaps he would do best to keep his mouth full at all times, he reckoned.

"You haven't given me any eggs," she murmured into the silence that had descended.

He glanced up at her to find her stare upon him, direct and assessing. She was testing him. "The omission was intentional, my dear. I've taken note that you never touch the stuff."

Her expression softened. "How thoughtful of you."

Well, he wasn't an ogre for Christ's sake. He may have been an inattentive scoundrel for the first few months of their union, but he did have eyes in his bloody head. He was beginning to get aggravated by her aloof air, and the feeling was a welcome one.

He deliberately ignored her, turning his attention to the butler who stood at proud attention. "Wilton, I should like to read my correspondence while I break my fast this morning. I find I've a rather busy day ahead of me."

He stole a sidelong glance at his wife to gauge her reaction. Her plump lips had compressed into one of her pinched frowns. Her brows were drawn together as well. Perhaps she was wondering what would occupy him for the duration of the day and take him away from her company. Not a blessed thing, but she needn't know it.

Pleased, he resumed eating his breakfast. He hoped she found him as vexing as he found her. She was warm, then cold. Told him she loved him, then wouldn't look at him. By God, he was confused enough on his own without her to further muddle things.

"Is something amiss, Pembroke?"

Yes, damn it. Everything was amiss. He was mooning over his wife and lying to her at the same time. He raised a brow and fixed what he hoped was a suitably wilting stare upon her. "Of course not, my dear."

He knew he shouldn't dwell on his subterfuge. Unfortunately, what had begun as a necessity now held much more dire repercussions. He had no doubt if she discovered his motivation for becoming a husband in truth, she'd wallop him in the noggin with *A Tale of Two Cities*. And once again take up her addle-pated notion of divorce. He didn't want a divorce. He rather enjoyed having a wife, especially one as delectable as Victoria.

The return of Wilton bearing a salver of various-sized envelopes saved him from further unwanted conversation. He dug into them with the same gusto he applied to his meal.

The sudden pallor of her husband's skin did not escape Victoria as he scanned one of his letters. She'd been watching him, consternated by his abrupt lack of interest in her. Odd that she'd become so attuned to his moods in such a short time. Perhaps odder still that she'd become so accustomed to expecting his attention.

She yearned to ask him who had written and why it had disturbed him. But their olive branch was still lying on the table between them, neither quite trusting enough to pick it up. Given his reticence in her chamber, she wasn't certain how far she could push him.

He glanced up at her, catching her gaze upon him. Her heart jumped into a faster pace at those blue eyes fastened on hers, bright and seeking. He cleared his throat, a habit she'd begun to take note of that happened whenever he was at a loss for words.

"It seems the duke has deigned to write me a letter," he said, his tone harsh.

There must have been something in the contents of his father's letter that had upset him greatly. She proceeded with care. "What does His Grace say?"

Will pinned a forced-looking smile to his lips. "He sends us his regards."

"That is all?" It wasn't precisely that she didn't believe him, but she was suspicious. Guilt nipped at her. "The letter appears to be rather voluminous."

She could see the letter was of lengthy proportions, the duke's dark scrawl visible as Will held the letter in question up to the light. She found it curious too that the duke was aware of her husband's presence in the country. She frowned as her doubts heightened. Unless of course it had been sent up from the Belgravia House. Perhaps she was overthinking it.

He folded the epistle with care and slid it inside the pocket of his jacket. "He also prattles on about his falcons or some such."

Falcons. Did he think her obtuse? No man wrote an entire page filled with nonsense about falcons. She pressed on, more convinced than before that he was hiding something from her. "What has upset you then? Perhaps you harbor a strong dislike for falconry?"

"Upset?" He raised an imperious brow. "On the contrary, my dear, I've never been happier."

She considered him for a moment. "You don't appear happy to me."

"But I am. The miserable old codger also writes that he plans to grace us with his presence." Bitterness laced his voice.

The duke had spoken to her on exactly two occasions thus far, once at a ball given in honor of her betrothal, and once on her wedding day. All other communication had been strictly conducted with her father. Victoria had been a bartered commodity, a necessary addition for the sake of the hallowed family coffers. Perhaps the notion of the duke's visit had distressed Will. Lord knew it didn't sit well with her. He was stuffy and had a way of looking at her that made her feel as if she'd dropped a glob of aspic on her silk dress.

Despite her reservations, it was her duty to play hostess to the man. The duke's arrival would likely send the household into an uproar. "When does he plan to arrive? I'll need time to prepare."

"A fortnight hence." Will couldn't have worn a more disgusted expression had he just bitten into a plate of rotten eggs instead of Cook's heavenly creations.

A fortnight didn't leave them with much time.

Victoria nearly dropped her fork. She stilled, plastering a pleasant expression to her face. "How delightful."

"How dreadful would actually be more like it." He muttered what sounded like a rather rude round of curses beneath his breath.

"He can't be all bad." Could he? She had to admit that as unflappable as Will seemed in all other matters, when it came to the duke, he was very much affected. Surely there was a good reason for it.

"You shall see."

She wondered again at what could have rendered her husband so cold, so hateful toward his father. Perhaps he would never confide in her. Lord knew he was adept at avoiding serious subjects in favor of other, far naughtier pursuits.

He abruptly dropped his fork to his plate. "I find I've quite lost my appetite. Would you care for a ride, my lady?"

Victoria wasn't precisely at home on a horse. Equestrienne had never been one of her talents. She hesitated. "I'm not certain I'm in the mood to be jostled about."

Of course, the opportunity to spend more time with Will was appealing indeed. She very much wanted to continue in their tentative pax. Perhaps the awkwardness of the morning could be mollified, at least in part.

"Pray take pity on me, my dear. I've had a rough morning." He gave her a grin that sent heat straight to her core.

The man knew how to make her bend to his whims. He was dangerous.

"Very well," she agreed after a bit of introspection. "I'll accompany you."

chapter seven

WILL HAD GIVEN HER THE MOST DOCILE MARE in the stables. The horse was so calm, in fact, that Victoria would have sworn she was sleeping on her hooves except that she kept plodding along at an exceedingly slow pace. Pembroke, meanwhile, rode a horse as sleek as it was fast. They'd only been riding for a few minutes and already she grew tired of having a view of his mount's hindquarters.

"Will," she called.

He stopped and turned back to her. "What is it, my dear?"

"I thought you said you wanted me to accompany you."

He frowned as she caught up to him and reined in her sluggish horse. "You *are* accompanying me."

"Not precisely." Her mare began nosing through a clump of grass, deciding it was time for a second breakfast. "I've been staring at your back the entire time."

"I've been told I have a delightfully broad back. I thought you may have wanted to admire it."

His tone was deadly serious. Victoria searched his bland

expression, trying to discern if he was having her on. She couldn't tell. Each day with him proved an altogether enlightening experience. Finally, he laughed, the hard planes of his handsome face softening. There was much more to him, she thought, than the stranger who had abandoned her in favor of living a wastrel's life in London. He continued to surprise her and work his way deeper into her heart. Drat the man.

"I'm teasing you, Victoria." He grinned at her. "Don't you Americans ever laugh?"

An answering smile tugged at her lips. "Of course we do."

He sobered. "I suppose I haven't given you much cause for levity." He paused, his gaze intense upon hers. "Let's dismount and take a walk."

Without waiting for her response, he dropped from his mount with effortless grace and reached up to assist her. His hands circled her waist as he helped her to the ground. When her feet were safely in the grass once more, however, he didn't release her from his hold. Instead, his hands lingered upon her, his tall form pressing into her diminutive one.

"You are impossibly lovely," he murmured, his head lowering toward hers.

She turned her face at the last moment, presenting him with her cheek instead of her lips. He kissed her just the same, but his grip tightened on her.

"Am I being punished for this morning?"

Victoria tore her eyes from his, lest she allow him to charm her into indulging in the passion flaring even now between them. She wanted to show him she could be as unaffected as he by their encounters. Of course, that wasn't at all true, but she had a suspicion that she shouldn't allow him to see her entire hand in the game they played.

"What have you done that requires punishment?" she asked in lieu of answering his query.

He released his grip on her waist with one hand and

gently touched her chin, forcing her to look at him once more. His gaze was blue, snapping with seductive fire and something indefinable. Penance? She couldn't be certain.

"I left you in haste this morning," he said lowly. "I'm aware I was an ass. I cannot make an excuse for myself, save to say that I meant you no insult. My mind was simply weighed down with weightier matters."

She raised a brow. "Weightier matters?"

He cleared his throat, looking ill at ease. "Estate business," he clarified with obvious ambiguity.

"Indeed?" It was her turn to raise a brow. "I was under the impression you haven't ever handled estate matters here at Carrington House."

"Devil take it, you're a prying woman," he groused. "Very well, if you must have it, I was overwhelmed by the realization that I cannot seem to get enough of my lovely wife."

She didn't think she believed that explanation any more than his first. But his words sent desire slipping through her wanton body just the same. "Somehow, I suspect you're mocking me."

"Not at all, my dear." His eyes darkened. He caressed her cheek again. "I wouldn't jest about that." He traced a path down her throat, stopping at the first fastener on her high-necked riding habit. "Bloody hell, you're always over-buttoned."

Victoria laughed at his frustrated observation, partially to dispel the troubling surge of want swirling through her. "It's the first stare of fashion, you know."

"Fashion should think a bit more about a man who wants to debauch his wife," he grumbled, unhooking the top button from its mooring. "There we are. Only eight hundred more to go."

"Pembroke," she protested, scandalized that he was beginning to disrobe her in the middle of the day, in the open air.

"I'm back to Pembroke, am I?" He continued opening

her bodice. "I shall have to remedy that."

Taking a fortifying breath, she forced herself to look over his shoulder. His horse was starting to wander. It presented the perfect excuse to regain her ability to resist him. "You may want to tether our horses first. I'm certain mine won't travel too far from her meal, but yours is another matter entirely."

"Damn." Wearing an aggrieved look, he released her and strode after his horse.

Victoria deemed it best to undo the damage he'd wrought upon her smart wardrobe. Quickly, she refastened her bodice. She watched as he secured both horses before turning back to her. The moment was alive with sunshine and possibilities. She had to admit he cut a dashing figure in his riding breeches. He was tall, lean and muscular. The intensity in his eyes made her heart kick up its pace.

He stopped a scant few inches from her, giving her a boyish grin. "Now where were we? You've done yourself back up. That's against the rules."

She tried not to smile as it would only serve to encourage him. "I wasn't aware there were any rules involved."

"Only rules of my making." He winked.

"You aren't a fair competitor, my lord."

He snagged an arm around her waist and dragged her into his hard body. "Is this the first time you've become aware of that fact, dearest wife?" He lowered his head, close enough to kiss.

Oh he was tempting her again already, the sinful man. Best to stave him off by any means possible. Her mind fogged. "Perhaps you should tell me what the rules are before I begin playing the game."

"I must say I've always preferred the element of surprise," he told her before taking her mouth in a crushing kiss.

Her arms wound about his neck of their own volition. She opened for his tongue, reveling in the sensual way he dipped inside her mouth to taste and tease. His hands slid up the small of her back in a possessive brand. Her resolve crumbled as if it were a ship being dashed against a rocky shore. She wanted him, and he knew precisely how to make her give in to her desires.

Victoria pressed closer to him, breathing in his divine scent. She returned his kiss with all the fervor clamoring to life within her. Somehow, it no longer mattered that they'd begun the morning badly. All she could feel was his powerful body, his knowing touch, his claiming kiss.

Dear heavens. What did he do to her?

He broke the kiss at last, making a muted sound in his throat. Her breathing was ragged, her stays cutting into her waist as she struggled to regain her senses. She clung to him, not wanting the embrace to end. He looked down at her, his eyes fierce, sparkling with naked desire.

"I'm beginning to regret I suggested riding instead of merely returning to your chamber." He sighed. "Let's take our walk, shall we? If we linger another minute, I fear I'll take you here in the grass like a common stable boy."

A mixture of disappointment and relief speared her. She took his proffered arm and started off with him. Thankfully, she'd worn a pair of serviceable boots. Otherwise, her shoes would have been ruined by the uneven, damp ground. At least she could maintain her sanity when he wasn't kissing her, she reasoned.

"It's a lovely day," she murmured, opting for a safer subject. And it truly was. While she'd only grown accustomed to English weather slowly, she was beginning to admire it for its dramatic, often mercurial nature. Everything seemed so much more vibrant, greener, and more alive than New York.

"Fair weather today indeed," he agreed, his tone light and affable.

One almost wouldn't guess he had nearly been about to make love to her in the weeds. But Victoria knew, and it still sent a raging fire through her blood. She tried to focus on the scenery, the lush trees and verdant fields. In the distance, sheep grazed in a pastoral setting. The result was quite picturesque, even if she continued to catch herself stealing sidelong glances at her husband's handsome profile.

"Where are you taking me?" she had to ask. He was guiding her down a path that led into a thick, seemingly ancient copse of trees.

"To the river, my dear." He patted the hand that rested in the crook of his elbow. "You've appallingly little faith in your husband, have you not?"

She bit her lip as she mulled over how to answer that particular question. The truth was that she had faith and yet she did not. Just when she trusted, it seemed she ought not to do so. He was a conundrum indeed.

"On second thought, leave whatever's rattling about in your pretty head unspoken." He sighed. "I can tell from your expression that it won't be anything I'd prefer to hear."

She cocked her head, considering him as they continued to tramp on. "I won't say it then."

"Good." His grip on her tightened. "Tell me something I don't already know."

Victoria laughed. "Have you anything in mind?"

"My dear girl, how can I have aught in mind when I don't know it yet?"

Another burst of laughter escaped her. He could be rather entertaining when he chose, and his charm seemed effortless. "What interests you? That is what I meant to say."

"Hmm." He looked down at her, his eyes dancing with merry blue light. "What of your family? How many siblings have you?"

She pursed her lips. He ought to have known. "I told you while we were courting. Don't you remember?"

His expression clouded. "Ah, yes. There are five of you, aren't there?"

"Six," she corrected, her tone tart. He hadn't listened to a word she'd ever said, had he?

"Just so." He cleared his throat. "Felicitations on your new sibling."

"Libby is twelve years old," she pointed out unkindly.

"Christ," he muttered, abruptly halting their walk to face her and take both her hands in his. He was very serious as he gazed down upon her, his face stark with masculine beauty. "I have a confession to make, my dear. I wasn't a good suitor to you. If you were speaking, chances are strong I wasn't listening. Pray don't hate me for it, but there it is."

She had suspected as much by now, but his admission nevertheless stung. "I don't hate you," she allowed, "but I must admit I'm not terribly impressed. Am I so boring then?"

"Not at all." He squeezed her fingers, trapped as they were in his large grasp. "It is merely that I was that much of an ass."

No point in saving him the shame, she decided. For the first time in his life, he ought to pay what was due. "You were."

He brought her hands to his lips for a pair of kisses that sent desire skittering through her. "Forgive me, my dear?"

"I suppose so," she conceded. "But when next I ask you, you had better be able to tell me that I am the eldest of six daughters."

"Six daughters?" He looked aghast. "Don't tell me we're to have all girls as well. I'll go mad."

The mentioning of their future children sent an entirely different sort of emotion washing over her. Good heavens. Even though she had reconciled herself to the fact that she was expected to produce an heir for his family, she hadn't truly given the notion much thought beyond that. She thought of their lovemaking the previous night and earlier that morning. Victoria was certain she was flushing cherry red.

She forced her mind back to the topic at hand. She'd been berating him, not mooning over him, drat it all. "Yes, six girls," she confirmed. "Take note of their names as well, since you ought to know them by now. There is Rose, Lillian, Edith, Pearl and Libby."

As she spoke their names, it occurred to her just how much she missed them. They were all younger than she in age but dear in their own ways. Sometimes, New York and her old life there still beckoned her with its cozy familiarity and the comfort of knowing she was well-loved.

"Right," he interrupted her thoughts. "Roberta, Laura, Edith, Pearl and Louisa." His tone was hopeful.

"Rose, Lillian, and Libby." She gave him a good-natured swat. "You'll meet them all someday, I expect, and then you'll be able to recall their names. I'm sure they plan to follow in my footsteps."

"God help them," he remarked, his voice drenched in self-deprecation.

"God and their sister," she said, striving to lighten the mood. "I know how to navigate the treacherous social waters on this side of the world."

"Thank Christ you're a forgiving soul," he muttered. "Lord knows I don't deserve you."

"No," she granted, happy he'd noticed but wanting to make him squirm just a bit, "you don't."

Rose, Lillian, Edith, Pearl and Libby. Good Christ, he was going to have a gaggle of daughters before he ever had an heir. If he even sired an heir, that was. He should have been suitably horrified. But the devil of it was, he didn't truly give a damn. If Victoria bore him a dozen daughters, they would all still be theirs, bright-eyed, flaxen-haired little girls to be cherished.

Damn it to hell. He was getting maudlin. He dropped her hands, determined to resume their walk without further sentimentality. He ought to have known better than to have brought up her family, by God. What was the matter with him? Had making love to her addled his mind? Very likely, for his cock was raging just standing at her side.

He'd thought his mad desire for her would dissipate, but

it was growing worse.

What to do? Right, he'd been attempting to show her the river before he'd gone hopelessly afield. He offered her his arm once more. "Shall we continue on in our walk, my dear? Have you seen the river here yet? It's something to behold."

He recalled splashing about in it as a boy on the occasions his family had taken up residence at Carrington House. They had come often until that awful last visit. His mother had lost a babe, another brother, and had succumbed not long thereafter to childbed fever. While no one had been certain whether the father of the stillborn had been the duke or the duchess's lover of the moment, the babe's death had confirmed Pembroke as the sole heir.

Thereafter, the duke had sent him off to Harrow. Carrington House had been closed until he took possession of it as an adult. And now, he was here, his unwanted-turned-wanted American wife at his side. Perhaps he'd overlooked precisely how comforting it could be to know that another soul was his mate for life. He found he rather enjoyed marriage after all.

"Are you well, Will?" Her concerned voice cut through his troubled musings. "Your face is suddenly bereft of color."

He realized he'd been gripping her arm with too much force, so lost had he become in his tumultuous thoughts. He took a deep, steadying breath, gazing down into his wife's sweet, heart-shaped face. She was ineffably lovely, her hair artfully piled beneath a jaunty hat, her lips wide and lush, her eyes greener than the grass at his feet. His cock surged against his riding breeches. What the devil did she do to him?

And he'd thought this a game. Bloody hell, he'd thought it a game he'd *won*.

"I'm not certain if I am well," he startled himself by revealing. Apparently, she had turned him into a milksop.

"What is it?" She slid a bracing arm around him, leaning into his side as if he could somehow soak up some of her strength.

He didn't know how she could be so open and kind to him after the beastly way he'd treated her. Even now, he lied to her still, while she remained unwavering in her belief there was good in him after all. There wasn't good in him. If there was, he would have told her the truth right then and let her choose to leave him as she ought.

Instead, he was too selfish to let her go. He put an arm around her cinched waist, holding her to him as if he could forever keep her there, although he knew he hadn't the right. "The river is beautiful, isn't it?"

Wide yet shallow, the river cut through the eastern corner of the Carrington House lands. It was one of the rare treasures of the property, a place one needed to know existed in order to seek it out. As a lad, he'd come here often, never imagining one day he'd stand here with his wife.

"It's lovely," Victoria agreed. "But you haven't answered my question."

She was a persistent little woman, that much was certain. He sighed, wondering how much he should divulge. No one had ever cared enough to ask him about his past. "Carrington House is where my mother died," he shared. "She'd lost another babe, her fourth or fifth, I think. It was too much the last time. She took fever and died."

"I'm sorry, Will." She turned to him then, taking him into her arms.

"She wasn't a kind woman, but she was my mother. Watching her wither and suffer was not pleasant, regardless." He held her tightly, burying his face in the soft, sweetly scented skin of her neck. Her embrace touched a part of him he hadn't known existed, filling his chest with warmth and something indefinably odd. He felt deeply connected to her in that moment, in a way he'd never known with another person, and it scared the hell out of him. But damn if he didn't savor it just the same.

"Does it hurt you to be here?" she asked quietly.

"No." He pressed a kiss to her throat. "Not with you,

my dear. You've transformed everything, it seems." He paused, lifting his head to look down upon her. Their gazes clashed, hers filled with sincerity and caring. He tamped down the twinge of conscience that told him to confess everything to her then and there. "Even me."

She reached up, cupping his cheek with her small hand, a smile brightening her face and rendering her even more beautiful. "Thank you for confiding in me. I hope I can help you to build new memories here."

Not long ago, he would've told her he didn't want to build new memories with her, neither at Carrington House nor elsewhere. Not long ago, he'd been content to live the selfish life of pleasure seeker, devoted only to enraging and embarrassing the duke. Not long ago, this was the very last place he'd imagined himself, and this ridiculous feeling of emotion swelling inside his chest would've been something he mocked and scoffed at.

Something shifted inside him then. The sun glowed overhead and birds chirped, and the river made the same steady rush he recalled from when he was a lad. It was as though time hadn't passed, as though nothing had altered in all his life, neither man nor nature nor beast. This day, however, was different. Everything was different.

She had made it so. She, his American wife who had attacked him with a book on his first night back, who had begun transforming his dilapidated ancestral home with her keen wit and motivation even as he callously abandoned her. She, who possessed a giving heart and a determination he admired. Yes, she was beautiful, it was true, but she was far more than her freckles, long gilt curls, and luscious curves. She was good and compassionate and forgiving. She was gentle, vulnerable, kind. So easy to crush. He had almost crushed the goodness within her once. He vowed never to do so again.

It wasn't escape he wanted. It was his wife, and not for any reason other than the way she made him feel. Jesus, the way she looked at him, as if he were a man worthy of her love. He was the least worthy man in all of England. But he wouldn't think of that. Not yet. He wasn't willing to relinquish his hold on their fragile bond.

He yanked her against him for a long, possessive kiss. "Let's begin making new memories right here, Victoria. Right now."

A sudden, loud crack pierced his awareness. Not thunder. Not a gunshot. A falling branch. He caught her arms and shoved her from him, looking up instinctively to find the source among the centuries' old trees on the riverbank. It happened so fast, the huge dead branch dropping from the sky above them. No time to think. He shoved her, hoping she'd drop safely out of the way.

There was another crack as something hit the back of his head, then an ominous thud. His vision went black. He dropped to his knees, felled by the blow, arms groping for her. *Victoria?* Where was she? He couldn't be sure if his lips moved, if he was capable of speech. Nothingness swirled up to meet him. He fell into the dark, gaping chasm, his last thought that he had to protect her.

chapter eight

ER HEAD THROBBED WITH A VIOLENCE THAT sent answering pulses of nausea roiling through her gut. What had happened? Where was she? Her eyes fluttered open to a blinding light that felt like a hundred splinters embedded in her eyeballs. No light. Too much. Too much pain.

There had been a figure hovering at her bedside, perhaps seated. Head bowed. The image was seared into her mind. Who? How? Blindly, she held out her hand, seeking solace. Comfort. Anything. She dared not open her eyes again, for fear of that awful, beckoning light.

Where? A hand clasped hers. She clung. Eyes closed, a whimper from her mouth. She could almost see herself from above, a crumpled ragdoll trapped and broken. How had this happened? Why? Her lips were dry and cracked. She tested a tongue that felt thick and unused. Water. She needed water. Who could fetch it for her?

"Mama?" she asked, holding on to that hand. But no, it was not her mother's hand, was it? This hand was large and strong, the fingers too long, the palm too broad. Her thumb traced a path. A strange hand. Not one she'd often held. Whose?

"Not your mother, darling."

The voice was familiar. Warm and low. Clipped and precise. A man's voice.

"Water." She didn't care whose voice it was. Not for the moment. Her throat was parched. She was going to be sick. Her thoughts were a hodgepodge, running amuck in her mind. She thought she heard the sound of a river. Rushing, gurgling, then…something else. A bang, a jarring. Where had she been at the moment of impact? Something had run her through. Her body had broken into pieces and now she would die.

The smooth, cool porcelain of a cup was at her lips now. A gentle hand cajoled her, lifted her, helped to angle her so that she wouldn't choke. For a breath, she forgot what to do and then, it came to her. The cup tipped, water sluicing into her ready mouth. Yes. So good. She drank greedily. Too fast.

The nausea was back, gurgling. Too much water. Not enough. She tried to open her eyes again. Her mouth worked. No sound. Too much light, she wanted to say. Draw the curtains. And then, who are you? Where am I?

No answers, it would seem. The cup returned, so too the steady hand at her nape.

"Keep your eyes closed, my love," he said. "The darkness is easier at first. Drink slowly. Rushing will only make you sick."

Yes, and she felt sick. Sick with pain. Sick with confusion. Who was he? Who, for that matter, was she? Nothing made sense. Victoria. Yes, that was her name. Had he said it or had she? Another sip of water. She couldn't be certain. Someone had said it.

"You'll survive this, my brave American girl."

Surely she knew the owner of that voice? So familiar. So haunting. Her eyes fluttered again. The cup was gone. The hand was gone. She felt the absence of that touch like a blow. Where? Who? How? Breathing hurt. The in, the out. Her ribs. Had they cracked? It felt as if she were under water now. Her head pounded as though a blacksmith from the depths of hell pounded upon her skull.

"You must survive this, damn you. Do you hear me?" Desperation tinged the voice now. "You will survive this."

She didn't know if she'd survive. Her body felt as if it would break in two at the slightest provocation. A whisper. A breath. Her mouth moved. She wanted to tell him. Whoever he was. Was he someone she loved? Nothing made sense except for the bitter liquid that slipped into her mouth next. Yes, delirium made sense.

"I need you too much to lose you now. Fight, my darling. You must fight."

Who'd spoken those words? Had it been she? Had it been the elusive figure holding vigil? A ghost, perhaps? Worse, a demon? The liquid was doing its work. Her mind was a cacophony of images and thoughts. Odds and ends. Bits and pieces. A man's face, handsome and earnest. Her husband. Dear heavens, he'd been there with her. Something had crashed down upon them. Hadn't he? Hadn't it?

"Please." Her voice now, thready and weak. Who was the shadowy figure? She had to know.

Dark swirls, a languorous slide through her veins. And then, nothing.

Will woke with a jolt, his back aching to beat the insistent throbbing of his head. It took a moment for his eyes to adjust to the dim light of the chamber and recall where he was and why. He'd fallen asleep keeping vigil at Victoria's bedside, her fingers tangled in his. The awful sound of the cracking branch returned to him, and then came the panic he'd felt when he'd come to and found her trapped beneath the heavy, fallen arm of the tree. Her skin had been ashen, her hair red with blood. For a terrifying moment, he'd thought her dead.

He'd fought to free her with a strength borne of desperation, had taken her in his arms, profound relief pouring through him to find her breathing and warm. Alive, thank God. He'd found his spooked mount, hauled her limp form across the saddle, and galloped home, his only thoughts for her. He'd been frantic, frenzied. Scared witless.

He still was, for she had remained virtually insensate since suffering the blow yesterday. How humbled he felt. How bloody foolish. He cared for Victoria, the wife he'd thought to bed and abandon. Perhaps it was the heavens' idea of revenge for his sins that he only realized how very much she'd come to mean to him mere seconds before she'd nearly been killed.

He squeezed her fingers, leaning over her to brush some of her unbound hair free of her cheek. Her eyelids fluttered, lashes stirring against her pale cheeks. And then he was caught in her vivid gaze.

She blinked. "Will?"

Thank Christ. Her gaze appeared sleepy but lucid, no doubt the combined aftereffects of the laudanum and her blow to the head. He jerked forward in his chair, needing to be closer to her. To reassure himself she was real and well. He touched her cheek gently. "You remember me, darling?"

"Of course." Her hand rose slowly to touch her head. "I remember everything. Why would I not?"

"You were not yourself, after the blow," he said hoarsely.

There had been a brief period yesterday, before the laudanum, when she'd been confused and in deep pain. She hadn't recognized him or her chamber, and she'd been thrashing so fitfully that the doctor had feared she'd injure herself. Will hadn't wanted to resort to the laudanum, but it had seemed the only way to calm her and give her the rest she needed after taking such a hard fall.

He was ashamed to admit that for a greedy, stupid

moment after she'd calmed into a deep sleep, he'd thought of how much easier things would be between them if she'd forgotten all that had transpired. Head injuries were known to cause memory lapse, after all. One blow to erase all the wrongs he'd done—wouldn't it have been rather tidy then? But just as quickly as the thought had come, it had been vanquished by self-disgust. What kind of a monster would rather have his wife gravely ill than own his sins?

Perhaps the man he'd been before he'd returned to Carrington House was just such a monster. But he was not that man any longer, and the time would come when he needed to unburden himself to her. Strip himself bare. Then she'd see all the ugliness hidden in his rotten soul, and she'd either turn away in revulsion or she'd forgive him. Either way the chance was his to take, and she was more than worthy of it.

"My head feels as though I placed it beneath a carriage wheel," she said, wincing.

"I've no doubt." His hands still tremored to think of how close she'd come to death. If the branch had been mere inches in either direction, it would have killed her. "You're very fortunate to have only suffered a concussion of the brain and some other bruising. It's a miracle the branch didn't do far worse damage."

Her full lips, still pale, quirked into a semblance of a smile. "If it had, you would've been rid of one unwanted wife."

"Jesus, Victoria. That was a poor jest."

She gave a small shrug. "Perhaps a blow to the head disturbs the mind."

He caressed her jaw lightly. "The doctor assured me that if you regained your senses today, you'd be fine." He turned to the side table and its vast array of accoutrements. Poultices, tea, water, laudanum, bandages. He hadn't allowed anyone else to attend to her. The servants had brought him supplies and left. She was his wife, by God, and it was his fault that she'd been standing in the trees by the river. If he hadn't been so caught up in the past, in his own memories and fears, he would've taken note of his surroundings, and he could've saved them both a great deal of pain. "Damn it, the tea's grown cold. Shall I have your woman fetch you another pot? You must be thirsty, darling."

But his stubborn wife frowned at him. Even in her weakened, pain-racked state, she could fashion disapproval as no one else. "You needn't wait on me, Will. Keats can sit with me. You look in need of rest yourself."

"No. It will be me or no one." He owed her that much. Indeed, he owed her far, far more than merely dancing attendance at her bedside. But for now, this would do.

"Will—"

"Hush," he interrupted. "I'm your husband. It's my duty. Would you care for a fresh pot of tea or some water?"

She stared at him, her expression indecipherable. "Water if you please."

Would that he could read her better. Whether it was the darkness of the chamber or the jumble of his emotions, he couldn't be sure, but something had shaken him from his ability to read her. He poured some water into a cup and handed it to her with care. "Are you hungry? I'll send for a bowl of porridge from Mrs. Rufton."

She took several long, lusty gulps of water before answering him. "No porridge, if you please. I dislike it intensely."

He raised a brow. "Porridge and eggs both?"

"I cannot help what I don't like." Her expression softened. "I've forgotten to ask after your wellbeing. Were you not hit by the branch?"

"I was and I've the devil of a headache." He rubbed the knot on his head ruefully. "But it was nothing compared to you. When I came to, I thought…" He hesitated, aware that he was about to reveal more than he wished.

She took another deep pull of her water. "What did you think, my lord?"

"Will." He took the cup from her. "You're drinking too much, love. You won't want to be ill."

"What did you think?" she persisted, her tone quiet yet demanding.

He met her gaze. "I thought I'd lost you, damn it." To his great mortification, his voice shook on the statement. Devil take it. The Earl of Pembroke did not cry. At least, he hadn't shed a tear in all the years since he'd found his puppy dead at the foot of his bed. Ferdinand. Odd how he could still recall how the mutt felt in his arms, all wiggly and warm. "There." He replaced her cup on the side table with too much force. The sound echoed in the silence of the chamber, water sloshing over the rim onto his hand. "Are you pleased now?"

"No."

He looked at her sharply. "Madam, in the last two days, I've been to hell and back worrying over you. I suggest you give me quarter."

"Quarter perhaps." She patted the bed at her side. "Won't you hold me, Will? I'm so very tired, and I won't be pleased until I have you nearer to me."

Hell. He'd do anything she asked. Anything. His mind was still reeling with emotion, with all that had happened. But this, her in his arms, he could make sense of. Gently, taking care not to jostle her, he slipped beneath the counterpane and pressed the length of his body to hers. She nuzzled into him with complete trust and a sigh.

"Thank you, Will," she murmured against his chest. "Thank you for saving me, and thank you for staying by my side. You needn't have."

He drew an arm around her waist, and if he clutched her to him more tightly than he intended, it couldn't be helped. She thought he'd saved her. Sweet Christ. Little did she know that it was the other way around. He found her cheek with his lips, bussing it softly. "Of course I needed to, my sweet. How could you ever think otherwise?"

But she had already fallen asleep.

Victoria didn't know how much time had passed, but when next she woke, Will had gone. She turned her aching head with ginger care and pressed her nose into the pillow to catch his scent. Spice and musk—the only sign he'd been there. That, and the pang in her heart.

He'd been concerned for her. His handsome face had not reflected his customary effortless charm when she'd first opened her eyes to find him at her bedside. She'd caught a glimpse of him without the mask he ordinarily wore, and he'd appeared haunted, his mouth set in a grim line of worry, his dark hair rumpled, purple half moons beneath his startling eyes. She hadn't mistaken the hitch in his voice when he'd spoken of finding her trapped beneath the fallen branch, either.

"My lady, you're awake," Keats said warmly, bustling to her side and cutting through her heavy musings.

She'd been so quiet that Victoria had thought herself alone. She gave her dear lady's maid what she hoped was a chipper smile. "Keats, would you mind terribly telling me what time of day it is?"

"It's late afternoon, Lady Pembroke, and if I may say, you're looking a sight better than you've been since your accident. You must be famished. Would you care for a tray to be brought up?"

"That would be lovely." Her stomach growled as if on cue, and she was pleasantly surprised to find that the incessant throbbing of her head had abated somewhat. "No porridge, however, if you please."

Keats frowned, worry grooves bracketing the older woman's eyes. "My lady, Lord Pembroke has us on strict orders to follow the doctor's advice. I'm afraid 'tis only porridge and tea for you until he says otherwise. Perhaps I can fetch you a warm glass of milk. He didn't say anything of milk, now that I think on it."

Just the thought of warm milk made her stomach roil. "No warm milk, if you please. Keats, where is his lordship?"

"He's returned to his chamber for a bath and a shave. The stubborn goat wouldn't go until I promised I wouldn't leave your side. All bloodied and stinking of mud from the excitement, he was, and refusing to do anything about it. He spent the entire first night watching over you. Didn't even sleep a wink, I daresay."

Victoria had to suppress a smile at Keats referring to Pembroke as a stubborn goat. It was true, of course, but it really was the sort of thing one ought not to call one's employer. Fortunately, Victoria was possessed of what some would consider rather odd sensibilities. She admired free thinking and candor.

Keats seemed to think better of her words, for her cheeks flushed. "Begging your pardon, my lady. I should not have called his lordship a stubborn goat. I wouldn't have done if he hadn't acted the part."

She couldn't stifle the small laugh that escaped her at Keats' grudging apology. Heavens, her entire body still seemed to ache with the force of the fall she'd taken. She wondered if she was one plum-colored bruise from head to toe.

"He does possess a rare *tenacity*, does he not, Keats?" she asked, mirth creeping into her tone.

"That he does, my lady," Keats agreed, fussing over the bedclothes, straightening them to her satisfaction. "There now. But if I may be so forthright, I have to say that I'm happy to see his particular tenacity being directed toward a good cause at last."

A good cause at last.

Yes, so too was she. "Did he truly stay by my side for— oh dear, how many days have passed now?"

"Three whole days, my lady," Keats surprised her by revealing. "Aye, that he did."

Three days. She recalled Will telling her she'd been unconscious for two days, so that meant she'd slept away yet another day. He hadn't even remained in her presence for more than three hours after their wedding vows had been spoken, and yet he had remained with her, the comforting warmth at her side, the hand holding the cup to her lips, the beloved voice urging her to survive.

Fight, my darling. You must fight.

It came back to her now in fragments. Will had been there at her side all along, the shadowy figure on the edges of her subconscious when she'd been in such devastating pain. He'd pushed her out of the way of the falling branch that day. One moment, she'd been in his arms, and the next, she heard a loud crack and there she stood, too foolish to move. He'd shoved her out of the branch's most direct path, even suffering a blow to the head himself in the process.

None of these actions belonged to a selfish man or a cruel man or a man incapable of emotion. He'd told her that she'd changed everything, even him. But that wasn't true, for he had changed himself. Something had brought him back to her, and she still didn't know precisely what that was, but she was grateful for it. Grateful for him.

Her stomach grumbled loudly yet again. "I must insist on no porridge if you please, Keats. Just a muffin, perhaps, and some jam? Yes, that would do nicely."

Keats grinned. "Yes, my lady. I'll be back in a trice."

Victoria scarcely waited for the door to close on Keats to throw back the bedclothes. She felt most unlike herself but good enough to have grown weary of lying about like an invalid. With a wince and considerably more effort than she'd thought the act would require, she hauled herself to the side of the bed, her bare feet brushing the soft carpet. Food would help to replenish her strength, she knew, but she wasn't about to lie abed waiting. With another heave, she stood on the wobbly legs of a newborn foal. She shook out her nightdress and remained still, willing the abrupt thumping in her head to subside enough that she didn't fear she'd cast up her accounts.

So much for being strong, she thought grimly as she

forced one foot in front of the other. Ah, yes. Walking now. She could do this. The nausea relented like an ocean wave being drawn back out to sea. She took a deep inhalation. Another step. Then another.

The door joining her chamber to Will's opened, and there he stood, more handsome than she'd ever seen him. He wore plain trousers and a white shirt without the formality of a waistcoat, and his feet were bare, his dark hair falling wetly to his collar. Their gazes collided. For a heady moment, it was as if the entire outside world was suspended. Only the two of them existed, their hearts beating in unison, their bodies attuned. He was her husband, her lover. He was the man she loved, and it was a deep love, strong and abiding. She'd thought she'd loved him before, but her old feelings were paltry compared to this new, all-encompassing rush.

"Victoria, what the devil do you think you're doing?" The irritation in his voice dashed away her maudlin thoughts. "Where the hell is your lady's maid? I told her not to leave you, damn it."

"I'm walking." She held out her arms and beamed, knowing she must look a sight with her stale nightgown, hair a wild tangle around her shoulders, and a wan face, but she didn't care. A ridiculous surge of joy coursed through her as she stood there before him. "I don't believe I've ever felt better, Will."

"Jesus." He frowned as he closed the distance between them and placed steadying, possessive hands on her waist. "She didn't give you more laudanum, did she? I expressly forbid you getting another drop of that poison."

"No laudanum, I can assure you. My head is aching ferociously."

"Of course it is." He began shepherding her back to the bed she'd just freed herself from. "You've suffered a serious injury, Victoria. You need rest. Bloody hell, I'm sacking your maid when she returns from wherever it is she's gone."

"You cannot sack Keats." She mustered the flagging

strength she had remaining and put up resistance. "Will, stop. I don't wish to be abed. I want to stretch my legs for a moment. She's fetching me some muffins and jam at my behest."

"You're to have porridge until the doctor deems otherwise." His fingers tightened on her waist, and even in her diminished state, the heat of him through the fine linen of her nightgown was enough to affect her. "You must return to bed whether you wish it or not."

"I don't wish it." Her tone was mulish but she didn't care. She'd been bursting with emotion, her love for him beating within her with the force of a heart, and he was doing his best to undermine it. "You're being a bully."

"A bully?" He looked genuinely taken aback. "Good Christ, woman. If I must bully you to keep you from injuring yourself more by gadding about your bloody chamber like you're on a promenade in Hyde Park, then I will. Have you any idea what these last three days have been like? I leave your side for half an hour, and here you are, ordering muffins and about to swoon."

Her head continued to pound, but the brightness of her spirits remained undiminished. She grinned. "Muffins shall always be preferable to porridge, and I wasn't about to swoon."

"You're deuced unsteady on your feet for a woman who wasn't about to swoon. You need to gather up your strength. I won't have you injuring yourself worse than you already are," he growled.

But she was undeterred. "Truly, I've never felt better. Your concern is misplaced."

With a long-suffering sigh, he bent and scooped her up into his arms in one swift motion. "You'll be the death of me, woman."

She looped her arms around his neck. Well, if he must be an overbearing barbarian, at least let him be one who cared enough to stay by her sickbed for three whole days. "I don't see any trees about, do you?" she asked, tongue in cheek.

"All I see is one lovely, frustrating woman who is about to settle down with a nice, warm bowl of porridge before she gets some more rest." He laid her gently on the bed and made a great show of arranging the covers over her.

Heavens, he was more of a mother hen than Keats. She caught his hand. "Will."

He stilled, raising his head to look at her with those blue eyes that seemed to see too much. "Victoria?"

"I would very much like to begin again with you," she said simply. "Starting today. I want the past to remain where it belongs."

A beautiful smile transformed his features then, softening the harsh lines of worry that had hardened his jaw and mouth. He touched her cheek with his free hand, then rubbed the pad of his thumb over her bottom lip as though he were committing it to memory. "I'd like that, sweet. I'd like that very much."

She kissed the pad of his thumb. "As would I."

Keats bustled back into the chamber before either of them could say more.

chapter nine

BUT THE PAST WAS NOT DESTINED TO REMAIN where it belonged. No indeed, and when the heavens decided to rake a man over the coals in retribution for his sins, they chose to do so in the form of the petulant opera singer he'd last thrown over. Will's gaze traveled over the woman perched on the edge of the striped silk divan in his drawing room. Her dark beauty was unmistakable, her fashion sense as impeccable as ever. The cloying scent of French rosewater clung to the air, and it rather made him want to sneeze.

What was the phrase? Ah, yes. *Curses are like young chickens, they always come home to roost.* Here then, was his curse. But she rather resembled a raven at the moment more than a young chicken.

"Signora Rosignoli," he greeted her coldly. "You must know you aren't welcome at my home."

"*Amore mio*, this can't be true." She rose and came toward him, her gloved hands outstretched. "I've missed you. Tell me you've missed me."

He hadn't missed her. Had scarcely spared her a thought,

engrossed as he was in his wife and his fragile, newfound sense of happiness. "If you had but written with your intentions, you could have been spared the time and expense of your trip, madam. As it is, you must leave at once."

"*Per favore*, do not treat me with so much ice." She swept closer, her skirts brushing his trousers, and laid a hand upon his chest. "Remember what we shared, my lord. *Ti voglio tanto bene.*"

He stopped her hand when it would have roamed lower, holding it in a firm grip to still further explorations. "You must go, Signora. I'll see to it that you have the means to return to London at once. Do not seek me out again."

"But my lord." She cupped his jaw with her free hand. "Look at me and tell me I mean *niente*, nothing. This I do not believe."

"Believe it." He caught her wrist, his patience waning. Damn it, he hadn't wanted to see her at all, but she'd refused to leave when Wilton had informed her he was not at home. He'd been shocked she would travel to the country to see him. Even more shocked she'd have the temerity to appear at Carrington House and demand an audience with him. More than anything, he hadn't wanted Victoria, who'd yet to come downstairs for the morning, to have any knowledge of Maria's unwanted presence. "You must leave, Maria. Our understanding is at an end."

"No, *amore mio.*" She pouted. "I refuse to believe it. What can this grim old place hold for you? Come to London with me. I'll do anything you want, *qualsiasi cosa.*"

Her sexual promises held no appeal for him. He felt instead oddly repelled, both by her and by himself. "The only thing I want you to do is leave. Lady Pembroke is in residence here, and I'll not have your presence dishonor her another moment."

"Lady Pembroke." Maria scoffed. "Your wife means nothing to me."

"She bloody well means *everything* to me," he snapped.

"Now kindly leave before my thinning patience deserts me entirely."

"*Mascalzone*!" She tugged free of his grasp. "I denied the Duke of Hathaway for you."

"Yet you're now free to pursue him," he observed drily.

"*Bastardo*! He already has taken the French nightingale as his mistress." She spun away from him and stalked toward a large portrait of the first Duke of Cranley.

He followed her, intercepting her before she could do any more damage to his family history. How had he ever thought to entangle himself with such a creature? "Damn you, Maria, do I need to throw you over my shoulder and haul you out of here, or will you go on your own two feet?"

Maria's thunderous expression eased suddenly as her dark gaze lit on something over his shoulder. A feline smile curved her red lips. "*Bene*."

Maria possessed a true bloodlust for the destruction of his personal property. For her to so easily be distracted from her quarry meant only one thing. With a grim sense of inevitability, he turned to find Victoria on the threshold.

She wore a maroon silk day dress with gold silk underlay and a velvet bow pinned neatly on her trim waist. Her hair had been schooled into an elaborate braid atop her head with a riot of curls falling down her back. She was lovely, a study in contrast to the tempestuous woman he'd been attempting to remove from their drawing room and his life both.

His wife held herself stiffly, the color draining from her pink cheeks as she took in the tableau he and Maria surely presented. Damn it to hell. "Lady Pembroke," he bit out.

But she either failed to hear him or ignored him, for in the next instant, she spun on her heel and left in a hushed swirl of elegant skirts. Somehow, her silence was more deafening than any cutting verbal condemnation could have been.

He turned to Maria. "Leave at once, madam. You've done enough harm."

And so too had he.

Victoria stood at the window in her chamber, staring out at the vast, sprawling acres that unfurled before Carrington House. This morning, its breathtaking beauty was lost on her. Her fingers trembled as she pressed them to her mouth, trying with all the determination within her to squelch the sob that threatened to rise from her throat. She would not cry. She would not shed a single tear.

Signora Rosignoli was as lovely as she'd imagined. Perhaps even more so, with her glossy jet hair beneath a handsome hat and a deep blue silk gown that emphasized her flashing brown eyes and her tiny waist to perfection. Even her voice was lovely, though she supposed that ought not to come as a surprise. The woman was a celebrated opera singer, after all.

When Victoria had come upon Will and the elegant, exotic woman in the drawing room, she'd been stunned. His hands had been upon the woman's arms. They'd been speaking lowly, their exchange animated and heated. *Damn you, Maria*, she'd heard him say. And Victoria had *known*. She'd known the identity of the stranger in her husband's arms without needing to ask.

She realized with painful clarity that doubt and fear weighed a great deal more than any falling branch ever could, and when those twin monsters walloped a woman, they were enough to immobilize her. The silken skirts and undeniable beauty of Signora Rosignoli was the embodiment of her worries. Indeed, the Signora was the flowering vine of every small seed of misgiving Will's actions had planted deep within Victoria's heart.

What a fool she was. What a pathetic coward. She'd stood on the threshold, taking in the scene before her, and so many witty setdowns had tumbled over themselves in her mind. Yet she'd not spoken a single word. Instead, she'd turned and raced back to her chamber to hide as though she were a scullery maid who'd been caught filching a silver spoon.

The door to her chamber rattled, indicating someone attempted to gain entry. She'd locked it on the chance he may tear himself away from his paramour long enough to attempt to placate her. But that he'd followed so closely on her heels still surprised her.

"Victoria." His voice was muffled, bearing an unmistakable tinge of desperation.

No, she wouldn't answer. Would not let him in. She hugged herself, eyes trained on the green expanse below. "Go away, Pembroke."

"Would you care for a scene? I'll break down the goddamn door," he warned.

"You would only do so at your own expense."

A loud bang echoed in the silence. Perhaps it was his palm slamming against the door. She heard muffled footfalls. Very likely he was returning to his mistress's side now. Maria, he had called her. Jealousy was an unforgiving beast. It made her hate the woman in the drawing room below. Just the notion of Will touching another woman in such tender passion, of doing to her what he'd done to Victoria…she couldn't bear it if he wanted to carry on with a mistress. She didn't care what was expected of the wife of an earl. Being a future duchess held no appeal for her. She had wanted only his heart, and that was a dear commodity indeed.

The door joining their chambers together rattled next. She'd locked it as well. Never let it be said that she was not a woman of preparation. "Leave me be, Pembroke. Go back to your strumpet."

"Open this door, Victoria." It was an imperious command, one that expected obedience.

Also never let it be said that she was a woman of obedience. "No," she called, not moving from her watch.

"Open. The. Damn. Door."

More pounding ensued. It suggested vehement determination. Dear heavens. Was that the sound of splintering wood? At last, she tore her gaze away from the window to find the door flying open and crashing against the wall.

He stalked into the room, his expression hard, jaw tense. In a breath, he stood before her, tall and fierce and handsome, the cad. She tipped up her chin in defiance and faced him, locating her mettle after all.

"You're quite the actor, Pembroke. First you played the regretful husband, then the charming lover, and now the angry brute." Her voice was devoid of emotion, and her bravado pleased her. "Tell me, which one of these roles suits you best? I confess I don't particularly care for the angry brute, but I suppose ruining doors is preferable to being a lying reprobate."

He caught her when she would have spun away from him, hauling her against him. "The only role that interests me is that of your husband."

Did he think her an imbecile? She dug the heels of her palms into his chest. "You cannot expect me to believe that after I came upon you with your mistress in the drawing room."

He refused to release her, his gaze pinned to hers as though he could make her believe him with the sheer vividness of his eyes. She looked away, fixing her vision on the window once more.

"I had no idea she would come here," he said. "If she'd but sent word, I'd have made it bloody clear to her that she was not welcome nor will she ever again be welcome. What you came upon was me about to toss the bit of baggage out on her ear."

Not half an hour ago, the *bit of baggage* had been Maria. No, he would not charm his way out of this. He could not bring his mistress into their home and hold her in his arms without consequence. "Of course you would say so now that you've been discovered."

"I would say so because it's the truth, damn it. Look at me, Victoria."

She refused to do so, partly because it hurt her heart too much and partly because he'd demanded it. "Leave my chamber. The door was locked for good reason."

"Please look at me." His tone had softened. "Would you have me beg? I'll beg."

He dropped to his knees before her, the action so unexpected that she couldn't help but turn back to him. He'd humbled himself, staring up at her with an expression she'd never before seen on his face. Contrition? Desperation? She couldn't be sure.

"Begging won't help your cause," she said without pity.

"Then tell me what will or I'll stay here on my knees before you until my legs go numb. I don't mind telling you I'm rather dogged when the situation merits it."

She wished he'd been dogged before he'd created all the wounds that seemed determined to keep reopening. "I don't know that anything can help your cause now."

But her traitorous heart made her picture him as he'd looked, worried and ashen-faced standing over her bedside. He'd nursed her to health. Hadn't left her side. The fortnight since the accident had been filled with the first real happiness she'd ever experienced in her married life. However, maybe happiness was not meant to persist. Maybe it was fleeting, life's way of lulling one into a false sense of contentment until the next runaway carriage came barreling down the road.

She wanted to tear her eyes from him and tell him to go to the devil once and for all, but something kept her trapped in his gaze and his presence. Part of her wanted to believe him. For surely he wouldn't invite his mistress to the very home they shared after all that had passed between them. Surely their time together had meant at least half as much to him as it had to her.

"Believe me when I say that I'm sorry," he continued as if he could sense her inner struggle. "I'm sorry for abandoning you here and for hurting you. I'm sorry for betraying our marriage vows. I've never been more bloody sorry in all my damn life."

This was not the first time he'd given her an apology, but she had to admit in spite of herself that it *was* the first time his apology sounded…genuine. Yes, genuine. Could it be possible that he actually was sorry for his past behavior? That what she'd seen in the drawing room had not in fact been a lover's embrace with that horrid woman? That he spoke the truth?

"I thank you for the apology," she relented. "But I'm afraid it's too little and far too late."

He took her hands in his, bringing them to his lips for a kiss. "If I could go back and undo all the wrongs I've done, I would wholeheartedly do it, and I'd spare you all of this. I'd have cast aside my petty rebellion against the duke and my resentment, and I'd have seen you for who you truly are, a woman who is kind and good and blindingly lovely. I'd have been a proper husband to you. I swear it on my life, Victoria. But the fact is that I cannot change any of my mistakes. You saw one of the worst of them below in the drawing room. Her presence here is my fault and I won't deny it. But don't, for God's sake, believe that I invited her here. I neither want nor need a mistress. You're all I want."

How could he vanquish all of her determination by dropping to his knees before her and giving her a pretty speech? She stared at him, feeling the anger lift from her chest, so too the hurt and the fear. Because he'd said exactly what she needed to hear. Because he was the man who'd given her pleasure against the wall of the music room, who'd thanked her for her work at Carrington House, the man who'd revealed his past to her, who'd noticed her dislike of eggs and the scent of her perfume, who'd saved her life and risked his own in the process. The man who'd held her hand as she lay bedridden and unconscious.

This man, the man on his knees before her who'd done all of those things, this man was the man she loved. She wanted to trust him. Wanted to believe him. God help her, if that made her a fool, then a greater fool had never lived.

"Stand," she commanded him.

He complied with effortless grace, towering over her yet again. "Forgive me, darling. I'm so sorry for everything."

Their hands were still joined, and she made no move to extricate herself. "Tell me why I should believe you now."

"Because I love you," he growled. "Jesus, there you have it. I don't know when or how it happened, and I certainly didn't even think such an emotion existed, but it's the only explanation for the way I feel. Christ, I'm a milksop."

Had he just said he'd fallen in love with her? Her dazed mind couldn't even comprehend such a sudden reversal of fortune. Of course, there was the possibility that he merely said the words to make her forget about the sight of his opera singer in their drawing room. *Maria.* There was a name she could never, in good conscience, like again.

She frowned at him, more bemused than ever before. "Why would you say such a thing to me?"

"Because I'm an evil villain out to bend you to my whims," he scoffed. "This isn't a sensation novel, Victoria. I have no motive other than that I want you by my side for the rest of my life, and I'm not about to let a lightskirt or my own pride get in the way of that."

Good heavens. She felt suddenly faint, as though all the air had been sucked from the room. "You love me?"

"I've begun to suspect that's the odd sensation I've been feeling of late." He gave her a self-deprecating grin. "You're in my thoughts night and day. When I saw you felled by that branch, I thought I'd lost you. And I knew then that I never want to lose you. I can't imagine my life without you in it. Will you marry me, my darling?"

She laughed, grateful for the reemergence of his infallible sense of humor in this weighty moment. "We're already married, you silly man."

"Are we indeed?" He caught her about the waist, pulling her against him. "How fortuitous, for now I'm free to ravish you."

An answering warmth pulsed between her thighs. She threw her arms around his neck and tunneled her fingers through his thick hair, holding him still as their gazes met. Before she gave in to what she wanted—what they both wanted—she would have his word. "Promise me you mean what you say, Will. Promise me that you love me."

"Of course I mean what I say." He feathered a kiss over her mouth, nipped her lower lip in a delicious little bite. "I promise. I love you, and I assure you that you're quite stuck with me now."

She dragged him to her for another kiss. He moaned, his large, knowing hands slipping down to cup her bottom. Too many layers of garments separated them. She longed for his hot, smooth skin, his broad chest against her aching nipples, his cock inside her. She longed for all of him and for everything he would do to her.

She opened for his tongue's possessive thrust into her mouth. She could only follow her body and her heart where they led her now, and she wanted Will more than she wanted to breathe. Desire and the thrill of his admission vanquished practical thought.

Only feel. His words once more returned to her, and they held more allure than ever before. Perhaps he was leading her astray, but the path to ruin had never felt so glorious. Hurt and doubt fell away. His deft fingers found the hooks of her gown, plucking them from their moorings. He peeled her bodice to her waist. It wasn't enough, not for either of them. The sound of rending fabric should have appalled her but it somehow had the opposite effect. Her corset cover and petticoats were gone, her silk pooled around her ankles. Her corset was next. All she had left was blind trust and the animal impulse within.

She pulled at the placket of his trousers. She needed to erase all memories of the awful Signora. Never again would she let another person come between them, she vowed to herself. Never again.

He broke their kiss, straightening to look down at her, his expression slack with passion. "Slow down, my dear. I want to make love to you."

"Yes," she whispered, need pulsing through her to her core. "Please, Pembroke."

"Will," he reminded her. "I find I'm ordinarily 'Pembroke' when you're vexed with me."

"Will." When her fumbling fingers couldn't seem to slide the buttons on his trousers free, she palmed his hard length. He jerked against her hand, his breathing hard. She knew a moment of gratification that he seemed every bit as affected as she.

"You're still wearing far too much armor, my dear," he growled, and whisked her corset, chemise, and drawers away in a blink. All she wore was fine silk stockings to her knees. And then he took her into his arms and carried her across the chamber to her bed.

As he lay her upon it, she reached up to frame his beautiful face between her palms. The slight abrasion of his whiskers was delicious upon her hypersensitive skin. He fused their mouths in a searing, open-mouthed kiss as he joined her on the bed after stripping off his trousers, underclothes, and shirt. Warm, wet heat pooled between her thighs. He brushed a tantalizing caress over her breasts, his thumbs toying with her nipples. She arched into him, sucking his tongue into her mouth, unable to get enough. He broke away to suckle the peak of a breast. His fingers went unerringly to the aching bud of her sex, working it back and forth until she was nearly mad.

"Mmm," he murmured, tonguing the taut nipple of her other breast as he gazed up at her. "I adore the way your body responds to me, my love."

He slid a finger inside her then. She eagerly opened her legs wider, thrusting her hips into his delicious rhythm. Another finger joined the first. She moaned, her fingers sifting through his silken hair as he tortured her responsive breasts with his mouth.

"I want you desperate for me," he whispered, his voice a deep, rumbling seduction all its own.

Dear heavens, she was, but he had rendered her incapable of speaking. She moaned again as he kissed a path down over the curve of her belly. He cupped her bottom and angled her to his mouth, gazing up at her across her pale curves. Their eyes locked. He sucked the nub of her sex into his mouth, working it with his tongue and teeth. The sight of him pleasuring her as she wore nothing but her stockings, his wicked mouth upon her most sensitive and intimate flesh, was her undoing. She knew she ought to look away, but she could not. Before, her skirts had covered him. She hadn't known how pleasurable it would be to watch.

His finger sank deep into her slickness as he worked his magic upon her with his mouth. It was too much to bear. She felt as if she were about to shatter into a thousand tiny, glittering shards. He tugged at her pearl with his teeth. A second finger slipped inside her, deep and angled. Oh, dear heavens. She couldn't bear another moment. She came undone, shuddering and crying out, grinding her hips into him with shameless abandon.

Yes. This—him—was what she wanted. Was everything she wanted. She shuddered with the aftermath. He rose once more, his powerful body atop hers, pinning her to the bed. She wanted to bring him the same fulfillment he brought her. "Your turn," she murmured, putting her hands on his shoulders and guiding him down to the bed so that he traded places with her.

She met his gaze, reveling in the unabashed desire she saw reflected in their smoky depths. She had no idea what she was doing, only that she wanted to bestow upon him the same raw pleasure he had given her. It was the ultimate gesture of her love for him. She lowered her head and took his rigid cock into her mouth. He was smoother than she'd expected. She ran her tongue up and down his length, tasting him as she sucked on the thick tip of his shaft.

"Christ, darling," he groaned after a time. "You're going

to bloody well kill me."

She smiled against him, continuing to suck and tease his arousal. It was wanton of her, she knew, but she loved giving him the same bliss he'd given her. Suddenly, he caught her shoulders and hauled her atop him. She was breathless as his cock pressed against where she wanted him most.

He guided her limbs so that she was fitted comfortably against him. "Rise up a bit, darling," he directed, his hands on her waist. "That's it."

With one swift thrust, he was inside her. She emitted a startled exclamation. Good heavens, she was atop him. She hadn't realized lovemaking could be done this way as well. It seemed she had much to learn.

"Ride me, my girl," he murmured, helping her into a delicious rhythm.

Her unbound curls swept down like a curtain around them. Their gazes locked as he surged inside her again and again. She found she rather liked the feeling of power her position gave her. Leaning down, she kissed him once more. Their tongues tangled, mouths sealed as their bodies rocked together as one.

Passion crashed over her like waves upon a shore until she could no longer resist the pull of the tide. She was swept away, helplessly overcome, her sheath tightening upon him in spasm after spasm of release. He pumped faster, moving deeper until he too let go. The hot spurt of his seed went inside her as she collapsed against his chest, thoroughly spent.

They were both silent for an indeterminate amount of time, the only sound their equally ragged breathing. Will ran his hand gently up and down her back in a soothing motion and gave her a swift kiss. Everything had changed for them now. But this was his final chance. She never again wanted to discover he'd been dishonest to her, and she damn well never again wanted to find one of his courtesans in their drawing room.

"If I ever see the Signora again, I swear I shall tear the false hair right from her head," she warned him. "You'll find I'll not be as forgiving now as I once was."

He laughed, his fingers tangling in her hair. "Now that is something I'd almost like to see. Your ferocity is one of the many reasons that I love you."

"Say it again," she ordered on a sigh.

"Now that is something—"

"No," she interrupted, giggling herself. "The other part."

"I love you."

She sighed again. She believed him, believed in what they'd just shared. How could she not? "I love you too, Will."

Tangled up in each other's arms, they went to dreamless sleep.

chapter ten

THE NEXT TWO DAYS PASSED FOR VICTORIA IN A state of utter bliss. She and her husband lingered in bed mornings and afternoons alike, making love to each other until she knew every inch of his body and he hers. It was all very much like a dream from which she had no intention of waking. Ever.

But their idyll wasn't meant to last, it seemed.

The duke had arrived, and his first order of business was an audience with Victoria. The summons came as a surprise to both her and Will. Afternoon light filtered into her chamber as she prepared for the undoubtedly uncomfortable meeting to come. Keats was putting the finishing touches upon her hair.

"Do you think my dress too forward?" She frowned at her reflection as she asked the question of Will, who had joined her in her chamber, similarly concerned by his father's odd request.

The duke had refused to greet either of them at his arrival. Instead, he had demanded luncheon in his rooms and a nap, in that particular order. She and Will had been secretly relieved by the respite, but now it appeared they would no longer remain so fortunate.

"I think your dress is splendid," Will drawled, meeting her gaze in the looking glass. "And if the old codger doesn't like it, he can bloody well go to hell where he belongs."

"My lord," she scolded, aware that as much as she respected and trusted Keats, they ought to at least hold up the pretenses. The duke was Will's father, after all. "You mustn't speak thus of His Grace."

He shrugged. "I don't like him, and I don't care who knows it."

She sighed, her nervousness threatening to get the best of her. Perhaps, she'd reasoned to herself, if she could earn the duke's respect, she could ease the troubled relationship between father and son. Perhaps there would be a peace between them, or at least a tentative melting of their mutual ice.

"I want to do well by you," she told her husband. "It wouldn't do if he thought me an uncouth American bumpkin."

"There's no danger of him thinking that, my dear," Will assured her, his visage grave. "None at all. I disapprove of his monarchal decree that you dance attendance upon him, you know. You needn't heed him."

"You could accompany me," she pointed out, made hopeful by her inner aspirations of reuniting father and son in semi-harmony.

His expression hardened. "No. Give the devil his due. If it's an audience with my wife that he desires, it's an audience he shall get. Never let him say we didn't bend to his whims."

She wished she could ask him why he'd grown so very serious and bitter, but she was ever aware of Keats' presence. Instead, she continued her preparations in silence, feeling as if she were the lamb being readied for slaughter. It was most disconcerting.

The duke awaited her in the drawing room. Wilton announced her with a severity she'd supposed only reserved for funerals. Indeed, there was something somber about the entire affair, she thought as she entered the room.

After having spent so much time in her husband's presence, she noted the similarities between Will and his father at once. They had the same dark mane of hair, though gray dusted the heavily greased strands of the duke's. His eyes were as blue and probing. The way he carried himself was stiffer and yet still reminiscent of Pembroke, with a signature aura of arrogance. The elder's whiskers, however, were quite pronounced, his mustache so large it nearly took on the appearance of a small creature.

The effect was almost laughable. She tamped down an inappropriate giggle bubbling up within her throat. Dear heavens, she couldn't make light of the august man. He held so much of her future within his age-spotted paws.

The duke made an imperious gesture that she supposed meant she ought to sit. Gingerly, she lowered herself to the edge of a particularly uncomfortable settee. The drawing room seemed somehow more imposing with his mere presence. She fussed with the fall of her gown, attempting to hide her nervousness.

"Lady Pembroke," he said formally when he too had taken his seat once more. "I understand you've flourished here at Carrington House."

She was under the impression only plants flourished, not people, but she wisely kept that opinion to herself. "I've merely done my duty."

"You have not, my lady." His voice was stern, unforgiving.

His assertion startled her. "I beg your pardon, Your Grace?" she was bold enough to question him, perhaps a character trait that was down to her proud American heritage. She had worked wonders upon the estate, and with an absentee husband no less. How dare he suggest she had somehow fallen short of his expectations?

"You are to provide an heir." He impaled her with an impenetrable glare. "You have not done so."

Goodness. She hadn't been prepared to speak of such a delicate matter with him. She'd never grow entirely accustomed to the English and their odd notions. She took care in crafting her response. "Your Grace, if you must be so indelicate, then so shall I. The fault of this does not entirely belong to me."

"I'm well aware of Pembroke's shortcomings," the duke growled. "It's his mother's blood he has running through his veins. But that's neither here nor there. I understand that he obeyed me for the first time in his misbegotten life and has returned to share the marital bed with you."

Victoria stilled. Will had obeyed the duke? Her entire body tensed as though preparing for a blow. She became hyperaware of her surroundings in that moment—the heavy breathing of the duke, the faint footsteps of servants beyond the closed drawing room door, the ticking of the gilded mantle clock. *Tick, tick, tick.*

She found her voice at last. "I beg your pardon, Your Grace?"

"You heard me aright," he snapped. "The earl has begun sharing the marital bed with you as I've asked. 'Tis half a year too late, but I'm counting myself fortunate that it's better late than never. I'll not have the duchy going to my cousin's spineless, wastrel fop one day if Pembroke doesn't sire a son. You'll do your duty until I've an heir, by God."

Her mind stumbled to sift and make sense of what the duke had just said. Pembroke had come to her because of an edict given by the duke? He'd *obeyed*, the duke had said. That meant everything she and Will had shared—every kiss, every moment of passion, every promise—had all been maneuvered by the hateful man before her. How many times had Will told her he had returned a changed man, that he wanted a new beginning, that he'd returned for her and her alone?

Surely he couldn't have been lying to her the entirety of

the time they'd spent together?

Or could he have? She pressed her fingers to her suddenly throbbing temples. The room seemed to spin around her. She didn't know if she was going to faint or scream. Will's words shuffled back through her mind like a deck of cards.

Victoria, I've missed you.

I've come back to Carrington House because I want to start anew. I love you.

Had everything been a falsehood, a fabrication meant to woo her into allowing him to provide the duke with a required heir? Dread skewered her. Yes, of course that was possible. He was the same man who had courted and abandoned her, the man who chased after lightskirts and ignored her with practiced nonchalance. She shouldn't be surprised by the duke's disclosure. She should not have fallen for her husband's handsome looks, charm, and knowing hands.

But she had.

"You appear startled, my lady," the duke observed. "Pray forgive me my plain speaking, but I've never been one to mince words. The plain truth of the matter is that Pembroke needs a male heir, or when he and I pass on to our rewards, the man next in line is an unsuitable country fool who will run the estates to ruin. Our family has possessed these lands for centuries. For them and the title to go to anyone other than the rightful heir would be a sacrilege."

She swallowed, trying to calm her madly beating heart and assuage the awful sense of betrayal overtaking her. "I do understand the need for an heir, Your Grace. You said Pembroke obeyed you. May I be so daring as to ask you what you meant?"

The duke's eyes narrowed in what she assumed was suspicion. "Forward lot, you Americans." He sighed, apparently put out by her lack of manners. "I've discovered that Pembroke requires an impetus for everything. I threatened to cut him off unless he returned to you and carried out his family obligations."

If her heart had been a finely cut crystal goblet, it would have been dashed into hundreds of infinitesimal shards in that instant. She wasn't so fortunate. Her heart wasn't an object, and it hurt with an intensity that blindsided her. She wanted to leave the drawing room. Her lungs felt as if they could no longer hold air.

This was far worse than Will's original abandonment of her. He'd told her he loved her. Lies, all of it. He'd connived and betrayed her all in the name of money. Her stomach gave a surge and she feared she'd embarrass herself before the duke.

"I'm led to believe Pembroke didn't share his motivations for suddenly returning to play husband," the duke unkindly observed.

She took a steadying breath. "He did not."

"Ah." He paused, considering her. "Surely you realize what sort of man he is, my dear. As I said, his mother's blood flows through him. He isn't to be trusted."

It sickened her that the duke spoke so frankly and with such disdain for his own son. Of course, it would appear that Will deserved it, but she found that notion comfortless. Little wonder he detested his father. The sentiment appeared to be a mutual one.

"I fear I'm unwell, Your Grace." She stood, her legs shaking beneath the layers of her silk afternoon dress. "Please excuse me?"

He watched her in stony silence, his gaze still sharp as rapiers. "You'd be wise not to allow your womanly sensibilities to impede your common sense. Pembroke will get an heir on you because he must. It doesn't matter how it's done, simply that it is."

If she'd been nearer to him in proximity, she would have slapped him, propriety be damned. She was shaken to her core, disgusted by Pembroke as much as she was his father. She understood his reaction to the duke now better than ever. The man was a toad who disparaged his own flesh and thought of nothing other than his crumbling empire.

She raised her chin, forcing herself to be strong and not allow the duke the last word. "You are wrong in that, Your Grace. There will be no heir, for Pembroke will never touch me again."

With that, she turned and beat a hasty retreat from the room. The duke called after her, but she ignored him. She'd had all the audiences with the awful man that she intended to have. Indeed, she wished very much that she'd never laid eyes upon him and Pembroke both.

Mere days ago, she'd vowed not to let anyone come between them again. How bitterly ironic that the only person who could come between them was the same man who always had. Pembroke himself.

It wasn't until after she was safely on the other side of the closed door that she allowed the tears she'd been withholding to fall. She hurried past Mrs. Morton, whose benevolent round visage plainly showed her distress. Pressing a hand to her mouth to stifle her sobs, she rushed to the privacy of her chamber before she humiliated herself any further.

Later that evening, the expected knock came at her door. She had deliberately avoided Will and hadn't gone down to dinner, pleading a headache. He'd spent the bulk of the afternoon off riding—no doubt an attempt to placate his conscience after his endless deceptions. Of course, that supposed he even possessed a conscience.

"Are you well, my dear?" he asked from his chamber, his tone concerned.

She didn't answer. Nausea churned in her stomach. A cold sheen of sweat drenched her entire body. She stopped in the act of pacing her chamber, hoping he would simply go away. She didn't think she could bear to see him just now.

"Victoria?"

Before she could even form a response, the door creaked open, revealing her husband. Of course he would have a key at the ready after last time. She hadn't thought of that. He wore a dressing gown, belted at the waist, and a worried expression marred the masculine beauty of his face.

It was God's idea of a cruel jest, she thought again, giving a man with a black heart the looks of an angel.

"Whatever is the matter? It's not like you to miss dinner." He started across the chamber, but she held up a staying hand.

"Don't come any nearer to me."

He stopped, a look of surprise replacing the distress. "What's wrong, my love?"

"I'm not your love." She took a deep, bracing breath, attempting to muster up the strength she would need to go to battle with him. The duke's revelation had left her shaken and weak.

"What are you on about?" He started forward again.

She retreated, eyeing him warily. "The duke told me the real reason you're here at Carrington House. I wonder that you sent me to meet him without fearing that he would. Perhaps you believed he would uphold your deceits for you, but it seems yours is a mutual enmity. He told me he threatened to cut you off if you didn't get me with child. That you're here with me out of obedience to him. I know that everything has been a lie."

Her voice broke on the last sentence, but she refused to cry before him. She clenched her fists at her sides, feeling dreadfully impotent. He tried to come to her, take her in his arms, but she pushed at his chest, refusing to be embraced. His face said everything she needed to know. It was true. All of it. He'd deceived her over and over again. *I promise. I love you.* Dear God, and he'd never meant a single word. The anguish was almost too much for her to bear.

"Victoria, I can explain." He held up a placating hand.

"No you can't. I don't want to hear any more of your

falsehoods."

"I came here for the wrong reasons," he said, gripping her arms to force her into stillness. "But I stayed for the right ones. I love you, more than I ever thought possible."

"You only love your own selfish gain," she snapped. "Unhand me."

"Calm down, love," he commanded. "By God, you've got to listen to reason."

Victoria tore herself from his grasp. "No. I won't listen to you. Get out now, or I'll scream and bring all the servants down upon us."

"You wouldn't." He reached for her again, this time taking her icy hands in his. "I should have told you myself, and for that I apologize. Surely one misunderstanding can't erase all that's happened between us."

"It wasn't a misunderstanding, Pembroke." She searched his gaze, trying to comprehend. "You deceived me from the first moment you came here. You said you were here because you'd been remiss as a husband. You said you missed me. I even asked you if you were here because the duke cut you off, and you denied it."

"What was I meant to say, Victoria? It's true that the duke cut me off. It's true that I returned here with the intention of bedding you and going back to London at the first opportunity. I had no choice when I wed you. I had no choice when I returned here. At least, that's what I bloody well thought, and I resented you for it. But I see now that I've always had a choice. My choice is you."

"Your choice is my marriage settlement. It always has been, and it always will be." She balled her fists into her skirts to keep him from seeing how badly they shook. "There was one reason for your return, and it was so you could keep living your wastrel life. God, I can't believe how foolish I was to believe you after everything."

His grip on her tightened. "I don't give a damn about my old life. All of this, all of what we've shared, has been real, Victoria. This last fortnight has been the best of my life.

Don't toss it away now over this, I beg you."

"It's you who has tossed it away." Bitterness laced her voice. She hadn't thought it possible to feel the depth of pain slicing through her now. He had promised not to hurt her again, but he had, and worse than ever before. "I trusted you, did everything a proper wife ought to. I ran your household, loved you, believed you when you told me Signora Rosignoli's arrival was a mistake. Even when I caught her in your arms, I still allowed you to persuade me it was all innocent. What a fool I was. Did you go to her after we made love?"

"Good Christ, of course not," he denied. "You're the only woman I want in my bed and you know it."

"No." She shook her head, tears streaming shamelessly down her cheeks. "I don't know anything any longer, for everything I thought I knew was a farce."

He released her, seemingly defeated. "I haven't been a good husband to you. I'm sorry. Sorrier than you know. I don't blame you if you hate me, Victoria. All I ask is that you not leave me. I can't bear that."

She stared at him, refusing to make a promise she couldn't keep, unlike him. Leaving him was exactly what she must do for her own sake. "Please vacate my chamber. I don't want you here."

"Very well." He offered her an abbreviated bow. "I won't linger where I'm not wanted. But listen to what I've said. I wouldn't have hurt you for the world."

"I wish I could believe that," she whispered, as much to herself as to him, watching as he walked away, leaving her well and truly alone.

Early the next morning, it came to Pembroke's attention that there was a vast assemblage of trunks being loaded onto his carriage. Still shaken from his confrontation with Victoria the night before, he stalked out into the grayish dawn light to determine what was in the works.

Footmen tramped in and out of the house bearing wieldy valises. His wife was overseeing the packing along with Mrs. Morton. Victoria was dressed to perfection, as usual, wearing a plum-and-black silk dress buttoned up to the neck, adorned with dyed lace and jet beads. His little American had blossomed into a true beauty to rival any English lady, and he didn't deserve her. He'd never deserved her, just as *petite souris* had never been a fitting description of her. She was fierce and kind and giving and trusting. All of the bloody things he wasn't.

Her gaze caught his. She didn't bother to offer any deference. Instead, she excused herself from the housekeeper and crunched to him across the stone drive. Her dashing hat made her seem taller. He affixed his stare to the plume of ostrich feathers pointing to the heavens. Christ. This couldn't be what he thought it was.

"I'm leaving you, Pembroke."

Or perhaps it could be after all. Bloody hell.

The wind blew ever so gently. Orris root. Her mere scent affected him. His jaw clenched, his eyes dropping to hers. Her expression was tight, her lips drawn into the imperious frown he knew so well. She was leaving him. Forever. His gut clenched, as if he'd just woken from a bout of all-night whisky drinking and he needed to cast up his accounts.

"Where are you going?"

"I'm returning to New York."

New York was an ocean away. He couldn't speak as the implications of her announcement became clear to him. She didn't plan on coming back to England. She no longer wanted to be his wife. Jesus, the thought left him cold.

"Then you shall be free to live life without the encumbrance of a wife," she said, interrupting his troubled musings. "Your family will, of course, keep everything. I'm only taking my trousseau. You may inspect the trunks if you like."

He didn't want to inspect the bloody trunks. He wanted

to have them hauled back into his home, damn it. "What are you on about, Victoria? You cannot simply run off to New York."

"Of course I can." Her voice was quiet, tinged with an emotion he couldn't define. "You don't want me anyway, and you never have."

"Damn you, that's not true." He realized that in his agitation, he was nearly hollering at her, and lowered his tone. "Not precisely. Initially, it was different between us. I'll own I resented you and treated you worse than a dockside doxy. But I've come to admire you. I cannot change what's happened in the past, but I can make the future what it ought to be. I want to be a true husband to you, Victoria."

Her eyes glittered with unshed tears. "I've realized that you are nothing but a liar, ready to spin whatever tale gets you what you want in the moment. Even your own father says as much. But I'm no longer your fool. You wouldn't even begin to know how to be a true husband."

He knew he'd lost the right to her respect. The man he'd been wouldn't have noticed the loss. In truth, the man he'd become was rather disgusted with the man he'd been, so embittered by his past that he'd been willing to use and hurt anyone to exact revenge. He didn't blame his wife for her poor opinion of him. He'd earned it.

"I've never claimed to be a good man. But I do love you."

She stilled. He held his breath, hoping his feelings would mean something to her. "Do not speak of love to me ever again," she all but spat, dashing his optimism. "You know nothing of it."

"You don't belong in New York." He clenched his fists at his sides, feeling utterly impotent as he never had before. "You belong at my side, as my wife."

"I don't want to be your wife any longer, Pembroke." She tilted her chin, her expression taking on the stubbornness he'd come to expect from her. "I want to go back to my true home, and this time I won't be dissuaded."

Deuce it, why wouldn't she listen to reason? They shared a deep passion together. He loved her. She'd said she loved him too. That had to mean something to her. Christ, but he'd bollixed this up.

"I know I should have told you the truth," he admitted. "I'm every manner of bastard the duke told you I am. Indeed, I daresay worse. But never doubt that I love you, damn you."

"Stop. Don't say another word." She shook her head as if she were trying to dispel his words from her mind. "I won't be your pawn. You may as well cry defeat."

He took her hands in his, determined not to allow her to run away from him. Their gazes clashed. He was as drawn to her as ever. "Tell me you don't love me, and I'll let you go."

A lengthy silence settled between them.

"I don't love you," she said at last, but she looked beyond him at the façade of Carrington House. "There, now unhand me."

"I don't believe you."

She tore away from his grasp as if his touch disgusted her. "I don't care if you do or if you don't. It no longer matters. I wish you a happy life, Pembroke. Truly, I do."

She turned and gave him her back, clipping back across the drive to Mrs. Morton's side. Another crashing wave of nausea smacked him in the gut. He was going to be sick, and Victoria was stolid, unwilling to be persuaded. He'd imagined that somehow he could convince her to see reason, for she couldn't leave him. Not now when they'd merely begun.

He turned on his heel and stalked away before he embarrassed himself by losing last night's supper in front of the wife who was leaving him and the servants who assisted in her flight. He only made it to the front entry before he lost the fragile grip he'd had on his control.

He'd simply allowed her to go. Victoria turned back for one last glimpse of Carrington House before the carriage ambled around the bend in the drive that would render it impossible to see. The imposing edifice stood stark against a graying sky, as arrogant as its owner. She'd come to think of its every tower, leaky roof and smudged window as hers to watch over. Over her months there, Carrington House had truly begun to feel like home.

Of course, if she were honest with herself, she'd acknowledge that it hadn't felt like a home until Will's return. But his return had been cloaked in lies, made only for his own gain and not out of any wish to be at her side. She turned to face forward, knowing there was no use in dwelling upon his betrayal. If she did, it would only devastate her.

Foolishly, she'd been hoping he would do something dramatic, perhaps chase after her, keep her from leaving. Instead, he'd merely stalked back into his sprawling country house without a backward look. A fitting end, she supposed, for a marriage that had begun and ended in deception. He didn't care. He never had.

Tears stung her eyes, and she blinked them away as best she could. Her lady's maid Keats sat opposite her as the carriage swayed, an awkward silence stretching between them. She knew it wasn't done to speak openly of private matters with one's servants, but Victoria had also come to realize that belowstairs knew far more of the comings and goings of its masters than the lords and ladies ever supposed.

"I'm leaving his lordship," she told Keats. What did decorum matter anyway? She'd had enough of the odd world of the English aristocracy. She longed for New York, for familiar faces, her younger sisters, her parents. She didn't belong here, and she knew that now more than ever.

"Oh dear, my lady." The kindly Keats appeared

genuinely concerned. "I'd heard whispers that something was amiss between you and his lordship, but I didn't want to believe it."

"Nor did I." She swallowed a sob rather than allow it to escape and further humiliate her. "However, I'm afraid he's left me with no choice."

They were off to London. Staying one more day beneath the same roof as him and the duke had been insupportable. She'd sent word ahead to her friend Maggie of her impromptu arrival. After all, she hardly wanted to take up residence in the Belgravia house where he'd kept his paramour. Even if she only intended to linger a few days while she planned her passage back to America, she wanted no reminders of her husband's indiscretions and intolerable behavior.

"Everyone belowstairs said he'd changed so much because of you, my lady," Keats offered. "He even took an interest in the running of the estate and gave raises to the servants who'd been at Carrington House for five years or more. My dear mother always said love is like a stocking that always needs darning. Are you very certain that whatever's happened can't be repaired?"

Victoria hadn't known he'd begun making changes of his own. That he'd cared enough to reward loyal retainers came as a shock to her. When she'd suggested it, he hadn't seemed to take the notion under much consideration. She knew too that he'd been poring over the ledgers and looking into repairs that were required in the east wing.

But learning a sense of responsibility for his land and people did not mean that he was a faithful, trustworthy husband. Though it was hard indeed, she had to keep that first in her mind. She thought of her maid's assertion that love was like a stocking and summoned up a sad smile. "You know, Keats, I do believe your mother was right. Love is like a stocking, but eventually it becomes too worn and you simply can't mend it any longer. Once it reaches that point, all you can do is toss it away."

If only tossing her love for Will away was as easy as that. She turned her attention to the slowly passing scenery, a muddle of pastoral beauty and lush green that was lost upon her. As the carriage swayed on, the clouds finally opened and unleashed a torrent of thunder and rain.

Will was devoting himself to the business of getting completely and thoroughly foxed. After he'd embarrassed himself by casting up his accounts all over the front hall, his pride hadn't allowed him to chase after her. No, instead, he'd found a bottle of fine whisky and had drained it to the last drop. He woke the next morning on the floor of the music room with an aching head and stiff back, still wearing his clothing from the previous day. Wallowing in self-disgust, he'd discovered a bottle of brandy in his study and begun all over again.

He tossed back the contents of his glass and stared with grim intent at the cuts in the crystal. She didn't want him. She'd finally had enough, and she'd gone. He couldn't blame her either. Damn it, he should have told her the truth when he'd first begun to have feelings for her. Telling her and making amends would have been so much easier before he'd allowed it to go too far. Maria's unexpected arrival had not helped matters, but he didn't fool himself on that score. The duke had been behind Victoria's departure. Damn the old meddling bastard to hell.

As he poured his third glass of brandy and soda water, the duke abruptly burst into his study. His blue gaze, so like Will's own, was cold as always, his face a mask of disdain.

"I suppose I shouldn't be surprised you're getting inebriated again," his father drawled, his voice laced with condemnation.

It was a tone he'd become accustomed to from the duke, but he wasn't in the mood to be harassed. He was a powder keg. One more spark, and he'd explode. He stiffened, trying to calm himself before he responded. Allowing the duke to see how deeply he affected him would not do. It was precisely why he'd been avoiding his father.

"Your Grace," he said, inclining his head but refusing to stand. "To what do I owe the pleasure of your illustrious company?"

"You have disappointed me your entire life, but this goes beyond the pale." The duke stalked across the carpet, stopping at the escritoire to slam his fist upon its polished surface. "You have had one duty in your miserable existence, and somehow you've managed to fail at it. I have it on good authority that you've bedded half the tarts of London and yet you won't bed your own countess."

"For once we're in complete agreement," he acknowledged tightly. "My wife wants to return to America. You can keep her gold in your blasted coffers, but you'll not be getting your heir."

"Nonsense. There won't be a divorce. I won't allow it." The duke slammed his fist again. "How was I to have known you'd lied to the chit? By God, you've never done anything properly. I should have simply married that American lightskirt myself."

The urge to land a solid punch to his father's haughty face had never been stronger. He stood, pinning the duke with a deadly glare. "Never insult my wife. If you even so much as speak her name ever again, I'll thrash you as I should have a long time ago."

The duke had a large stature as well, but his muscled form had withered with age. There was no doubt that in a physical match, Will would be the victor. His father knew it. He stilled, surprise evident in his expression. It was the first time Pembroke had ever stood up to his father. The weight he'd carried with him his entire life lifted. He felt light. Liberated.

"You dare to threaten me?" The duke raised an imperious brow.

"I dare much where you're concerned," he assured him,

a new sense of confidence soaring within him. "You've done enough damage here. I'll right the wrongs I've done, and if I have anything to say about it, you'll have your blessed heir. But that's only because I want to start a family with Victoria. I'll not countenance any more meddling or disrespect, not from you or anyone else."

"Who do you think you are to speak to me thus?" the duke demanded, sputtering.

"I'm your bloody son." Something that had bothered him for years returned to him then in that moment of rebellion, and he had to know. "Whilst we're throwing all the wood onto the fire, tell me one thing, Your Grace. Who killed my puppy? I was a stripling and my only comfort in the world was that damn dog."

His father's expression clouded with uncontrived confusion. "Puppy? I haven't the time to worry about your mongrels, Pembroke."

It had been his mother, then. After all these years, he had the truth. He supposed he shouldn't be surprised, but the revelation made his mouth go dry. He thought of the six-year-old boy he'd been, longing for affection from a broken, angry woman. That boy was now a man who'd treated his wife every bit as poorly as he'd once been treated. How could he have willingly visited that pain upon another? Shame was a breathtaking thing.

A new resolve overcame him. He'd spent his time enraging the duke with one scandal after the next. He'd wasted years on hollow retribution. But revenge didn't matter. He'd never change his father, never undo the damage of the past. But he could move forward. He could choose love instead of hate. The time had come for him to be a man. He had to win back Victoria. Without her, his life was an empty husk.

His mind made up, he strode past his startled father.

"Where the devil are you going?" the duke called after him, clearly consternated.

"To get my wife," he returned over his shoulder, not bothering to glance back at his father. The past was where it belonged, and the only future he wanted had Victoria in it. He had to earn her trust again. There was no other course.

chapter eleven

"OH DEAR."

Victoria glanced up from the book she'd been unenthusiastically reading in Maggie's cheery London drawing room. Her friend had just burst into the room in a riot of pinned red curls and violet silks, wringing her hands, her countenance quite vexed. Nothing could detract from Maggie's vibrant loveliness, Victoria thought with not a bit of envy.

She snapped the volume in her lap closed, not bothering to mark the page. As distractions went, it had served to be an exceedingly poor one. She frowned as her friend began pacing across the polished floor as if she'd just had word of a death in the family. "What is it, Maggie?"

"Forgive me, my dearest." Maggie pressed a hand to her mouth, looking ill. "I don't know how this has happened."

Victoria stood at once, a growing knot of worry in her stomach. "Whatever can be the matter? Surely you've done nothing that requires my forgiveness."

"I have not," Maggie hastened to assure her, stopping in her frantic motions. "But someone has."

"I can take no more suspense, Maggie." She braced herself for the news. "What can it be?"

"Pembroke," Maggie finally revealed. Even her carefully wrought coiffure was coming undone in her fervor. "I'm afraid he's come here and he's demanding to see you."

Welled-up emotion gave a sudden pang in her chest. For the past three days, she'd vacillated between anger and longing for him. She'd halfheartedly waited for him to turn up with his charming grin and melting kisses. She'd even had a dream her first night in London that he'd come for her and begged her forgiveness. It had been so real that she'd woken and looked for him in bed beside her. But reality had intruded with the glaring light of dawn, and she'd been alone in a strange bed, still betrayed and broken.

Now he had come, just when she'd abandoned the last shred of hope she still clung to that their love could be darned after all. She pressed a hand to her recklessly galloping heart. What to do?

"Has the butler told him I'm not at home?" she asked, trying to sort through the hodgepodge of her confused feelings. She didn't think she could see him now without crumbling. He had hurt her so very deeply.

"He has." Maggie grimaced. "The earl refuses to leave. He has said he will remain until you return. I'm sure I've never heard of anything so forward. Our poor butler hasn't an inkling what to do, and I'm afraid the footmen aren't burly enough to successfully remove him."

Of course Will would not bow to social custom. Of course he would be arrogant and demanding. Of course he would not leave. A reasonable man, knowing how betrayed she must feel by his deception, would have mercy and grant her some space. A reasonable man would not follow her to London and barge into her safe haven.

But the Earl of Pembroke was not a reasonable man. Nor was he a man worthy of her love. How foolish she'd been to allow him to deceive her and misuse her again and again. She couldn't, for her own sanity and well-being, allow him to charm his way back into her good graces once more.

"What am I to do, Victoria?"

Before she could answer, the drawing room door burst open. Maggie's harried-looking butler attempted to announce Pembroke while Will simply stalked into the room as if he belonged there. His gaze ensnared hers and her traitorous body went weak. She shot to her feet in an unsteady lack of grace, her forgotten book sliding to the floor with a thud her mind scarcely registered. Crossing her arms over her chest, she faced him. Her stomach tightened and her heart seemed a physical ache within her breast.

"Ah, I suspected you were hiding from me, my dear," he said, his voice as smooth as fresh butter.

Poor Maggie appeared to be having apoplexy. Her face had grown red in her agitation. She hurried toward him like a hornet whose nest had been trampled, out to sting. "My lord, you cannot simply barge about in my home."

He stopped and bowed, ever the sophisticated gentleman. "Pray accept my apologies, my lady. It is simply that I am overcome with love of my wife and I can't bear to spend another second without her. I'm sure you understand."

Victoria frowned at more of his silver-tongued niceties. He didn't love her. How could he, and treat her as he had? She was rigid as he strode to her, his eyes fastened to her as if memorizing the mere sight of her. She knew it for the act it was, and she was determined to remain unaffected.

Maggie was sputtering. "Your wife is seeking refuge from you, my lord."

"I am well aware of that." He caught Victoria's hands in his and raised them to his lips for a fervent kiss. "And I don't blame her one whit."

"You don't?" Victoria asked, her brow furrowed.

"You don't?" Maggie echoed.

"Not at all." Will still held her hands in a tight grasp, his intense eyes never straying from her. "I've been a complete scoundrel to her. I don't deserve her as my wife. I've abandoned her, lied to her, and hurt her, and for that I shall never forgive myself." He paused. "But I will also never forgive myself if I let her go, for you see, she is the very best part of my life."

She wanted to believe those words, fool that she was. Longed to believe them, just as she had so many other words that had rolled from his facile tongue. So many words that had dashed into meaningless promises.

"You certainly didn't act as if I was," she pointed out.

"Lady Sandhurst," he said, his gaze never leaving hers. "Would you mind terribly giving us some privacy?"

"Oh my." Maggie sounded breathless. Victoria cast a glance her friend's way to find that she was watching the scene unfold, pie-eyed. "I suppose so, my lord. That is, if it is acceptable to Victoria."

"I'll be fine," she assured Maggie, even though she wasn't sure of the veracity of her own words. In truth, she didn't know what to expect of Will, what to expect of herself. Seeing him again shook her. What he'd said shook her.

When they were alone, the drawing room door safely closed on curious ears, he pulled her into his strong body for an embrace. She held herself stiffly, her arms at her sides, as he pressed her tightly to him. He buried his face in her hair on a deep inhalation, as if he were drinking in her scent.

"By God, I've missed you," he murmured. "I know you don't owe me anything at all, but please, Victoria, listen to what I have to say."

"I don't know if I can." As admissions went, it was completely honest, bereft of any trappings. She had never been good at girding herself against him.

"I'm begging you, my love." He pressed a kiss to the top of her head, holding her with such ferocity that it was almost painful. "Please."

She loved the way he held her. Not returning his embrace felt somehow wrong. She had to force herself to recall the gravity of what he'd done. He was a man she could not trust and had shown that to her again and again.

She summoned her inner strength and pulled back to look at him, searching his gaze. "I needn't listen to anything you have to say."

"You are entitled to your good opinion, but before you refuse me, think upon this." His beautiful face was taut with an emotion she couldn't define. "What have I to gain in seeking you out now? You've already given me my freedom. Should a divorce occur, my family will keep your dowry. I'm young enough to remarry and try for an heir to please my father. I don't need you, Victoria."

His proclamation startled her. It hadn't been what she expected to hear, and she had to confess, if only to herself, that what he said possessed a ring of truth. If they were to divorce, or perhaps even annul their union, he would be free to remarry. In time, the scandal would dim, and he was the heir of a duke after all. The money his family had needed was already theirs. He didn't need her any longer, it seemed.

"I don't need you," he said again, tipping up her chin in that way that had become so familiar and beloved to her. "Except that without you, my life has no meaning. I was an aimless blackleg, with no thought for the future or my responsibilities, no care for anyone, including myself. And then I came to you in the country. You were beautiful and strong. You had transformed Carrington House, won over the servants, and I couldn't get enough of you. I discovered I'd married a striking, intelligent, caring force of a woman who somehow saw the best in my blighted soul when everyone else believed it had no redeemable qualities."

His words left her stricken, partially because she was afraid to believe them, and partially because she knew no one could put on such a skilled performance. There remained many questions, however, that needed asking. "Why would you lie to me? Why not tell me the truth?"

"I was in too deep," he said without hesitation, his gaze never wavering. "By the time I realized how much I cared for you, I was too afraid to admit to you that I wasn't the good husband seeking redemption that you thought me to be. I didn't want you to hate me or to leave me. If I could go back and erase the damage, tell you when I ought to have, know that I would. There's at least a hundred things in my life that I'd do differently, given half the chance. But I can't. All I can do is promise to do better in future. I give you that promise now, my love."

It was what she needed to hear. But the inundation of his revelations was too great. She was besieged, her mind trying to sort through the particulars of what he'd told her, her heart wanting to throw herself immediately into his arms.

"I can't make a decision now," she said, trying desperately to hold on to her fleeing sense of self-preservation. "I need time, Pembroke, time to think about all you've said."

He released a deep breath, closing his eyes for a moment. She was shocked that he was openly showing such depth of emotion. He had always been filled with skillful lovemaking, sensual smiles, and teasing to deflect from the seriousness of the moment. He had never been this open, this vulnerable.

"I understand, my dear." He brought her hands to his lips for one last, lingering kiss. "Thank you. I shall give you all the time you need, but I'm afraid I cannot stay away from you. I'll return every day until you reach your determination."

He would return every day? Good heavens. Her ability to resist him would be worn thin in no time if she had to see him each day. Yet she had to admit that some small, rebellious part of her wanted that to happen. She wanted nothing more than for him to prove himself to her. She had resigned herself to the fact that, regardless of what he had done, she would never love another man as she loved Will.

"Very well," she agreed.

"Until tomorrow, my love." He hesitated. "May I kiss you?"

She wanted nothing more than to feel his mouth upon hers, but her common sense told her she ought not to tempt it. "No," she denied at last. "You may not."

He nodded. "I understand."

And with a bow, he took his leave.

"Are you going to forgive him?"

The question, asked by Maggie over breakfast, gave Victoria a start. She glanced up her plate and the food she'd been toying with but not eating. Blood sausages had never held any appeal for her, but she had to admit she hadn't had much appetite over the last week.

"I'm not certain," she murmured. "So much has come to pass between us, and it's all left me hopelessly confused, Maggie."

Maggie sent her a commiserating smile. "I know, my dear. You have to admit he's been incredibly attentive. His actions seem to be those of a man desperately in love. I confess I'm rather jealous. I wish Sandhurst looked upon me the way Pembroke does you." She sighed, staring out the window into the busy London morning. "On second thought, I wish Sandhurst would look upon me at all."

Poor Maggie. Her husband the marquis was in love with Lady Billingsley and made no secret of it, carrying on an affair with the woman despite his relatively new marriage. Victoria had only met him but once, and he had been polite but frigid. He did not seem to be a particularly kind man, and Maggie certainly deserved a better husband.

Victoria forced her mind to her own husband. Maggie was right. Pembroke had arrived each day for the last sennight, paying her careful, polite visits in the presence of Maggie. He was charming as ever, incredibly solicitous, handsome to a fault. She suspected he'd even won her friend over with his undeniable magnetism. But though her resolve was weakening, she was still left more conflicted than ever.

She missed the life they had begun together, that much was irrefutable. Of course she missed sharing his bed, the incredible pleasure he gave her. She longed for his teasing smiles, his witty sense of humor. Still, hidden inside her was a desperately frightened heart.

"I'm scared," she admitted to her friend.

"That's to be expected, dear heart," Maggie said. "But nothing in life is worthwhile if it's easy."

As her friend's words sank into her mind, the butler reappeared to announce Pembroke's daily arrival. He awaited her in the drawing room. She took a deep breath. "Will you come with me, Maggie?"

"Not today, I think," her friend said with a sly smile. "It's time you met him on your own."

Perhaps Maggie was right, she thought as she stood, abandoning her barely eaten breakfast. Love was worthwhile, and she still loved Will, despite their troubled past. But was she ready to forgive him? Did she dare?

Victoria entered the drawing room to discover her husband had not entirely come on his own. It appeared he had also brought a study's worth of documents with him. He had spread an assortment of papers all over a *Louis Quinze* table.

"Darling," he greeted her, looking up from the act of shuffling through a sheaf of documents. He had an unusually severe air this morning, no sign of his customary teasing grin. "You are looking beautiful as ever this morning."

She was instantly on edge. "Thank you, but what in heaven's name is all this?"

"Legal papers prepared by my solicitor. Come and have a look." He waved her onward. "I hope they will hold some meaning for you."

Wary, she crossed the room to his side. His familiar scent

teased her senses. She couldn't help but notice how very gorgeous he appeared. She longed to fall into his arms, fall back into the life they had tentatively begun together. Forcing her feelings of longing to abate, she glanced down at the papers he had brought for her.

She quickly skimmed over them, not certain she was reading them correctly. "Can this be what I think it is?"

"I've renounced my claim upon your marriage settlement," he confirmed. "The remainder of the portions of the funds I was to receive has now been relinquished in full to the duke. There's no more threat of him cutting me off. I've cut the purse strings myself."

Could it be true? Her heart beat faster as she took up the documents for a closer inspection. Yes, she realized, it was true. He had truly forfeited his wealth, the one cause that had originally sent him back to Carrington House to woo her in the first place.

She looked back to him, a hand pressed to her furiously racing heart. "Why would you do such a thing?"

"To prove to you that it's only you I want. The rest can go straight to bloody hell as far as I'm concerned." He paused, his vulnerability reflected in his tense expression as he raked a hand through his dark hair. "There's nothing that can come between us now. My father has no hold upon me. Money has no hold upon me. I would have turned over the entail to him as well were it possible, but my solicitor assures me it's binding and old as the proverbial hills."

The gesture left her speechless. She had never expected something so drastic from him. A wild surge of love hit her, strong enough to bring tears to her eyes. It was too much for her to process. She couldn't have been more overwhelmed.

"Don't say anything yet," he continued, his brow furrowed as if he believed she would still reject him. "We'll need funds of our own, but I've thought this through. With your help, we can make the Carrington House estate profitable enough to live comfortably for the rest of our lives. It may not be the life to which you've been accustomed, but it will be ours."

Theirs.

She couldn't imagine anything she wanted more than to be free to love him without the encumbrances that had wrought havoc upon their union. "Are you very sure, Will?"

His eyes were steady upon hers. "I've never been more sure of anything in my life." He closed the distance between them then, slipping his arms round her waist and securing her to him. "I've also sent word to your parents, inviting them to join us in the country. I hope it wasn't too forward of me, but I've suggested they bring your sisters, Rose, Lillian, Edith, Pearl and Libby."

She reached up to trace the strength of his jaw, a tentative wonder unfurling within her. "You remembered all their names," she murmured, truly touched by both the gesture and that he had troubled himself to recall each sister's name.

His grin appeared in full force then. "The woman I love told me I ought to know."

"Oh Will." She felt suddenly weightless and breathless all at once. "I love you too."

He held her closer, angling his head down so that their noses nearly brushed. "Thank Christ. I'd begun to fear you no longer did."

"I could never stop loving you." She slid her palm up to cup his cheek. "No matter how hard I might have tried."

"Nor I you. Believe me, falling in love with my wife was the last thing I wanted." He paused, his lips achingly near to hers, his breath a hot invitation on her mouth. "I didn't even think it possible. But now I can't bear to live without you. I love you so much it bloody well hurts."

She laughed at his pained pronouncement. "I feel the same way, my love."

His teasing air returned. "It's been a week since I've kissed you, and I fear I may soon perish with wanting."

She grinned at him. "Then what are you waiting for?"

"Ah darling." His mouth finally claimed hers, the kiss possessive and deep. When he broke away, they were both breathless. "Marry me, my love?"

She giggled, pressing another kiss to his beloved lips. "We're already married, you silly man, and I couldn't be happier."

His expression turned wicked. "Then let's go home to Carrington House. I can't wait to undo all those damned buttons."

His naughty words sent desire through her. It had been far too long. "I should like nothing better," she said.

And hand in hand, they traveled out of the drawing room and into a dazzling new future together.

epilogue

One year later

"WE'VE DONE IT, MY LOVE." Will slid his arm around Victoria's waist, drawing her in a snug embrace to his side. Before them stood the result of their mutual hard work and determination: a brand new roof on the east wing of Carrington House. He couldn't have imagined ever gazing upon the old stone heap of his youth with pride or—even more shockingly—with such sated happiness.

But he was.

And it was all because of her.

She threw her arms around his middle and gazed up at him, her green eyes bright enough to rival the summer grass. How was it possible that she was even more lovely now than ever? A year of marital bliss had blessed her with a radiance that not even the dreary country weather could dim. "*You've* done it, Will," she corrected him gently, "and I'm ever so proud of you."

His heart squeezed in his chest at her praise. He'd be strutting about like a damn peacock for the remainder of the day just knowing that she was proud of him. But even so, this particular victory was not his alone. It was theirs, meant to be shared and savored together.

He caught her chin between his thumb and forefinger, unable to resist a swipe of his thumb over her full lower lip. "No, darling, we've done it together. Without you and your father, I couldn't have raised the funds for this endeavor, and we both know it. There's no shame in putting thanks where it's due."

"I'll be forever grateful for the months that we spent in New York." A sensual smile of remembrance turned up the corners of her mouth. "My father was more than happy to have you at his side. And I was more than happy for the nights. After all, that precious time is what gave us Alistair."

Victoria's large, boisterous family had visited Carrington House as promised, and during that time he'd developed an unlikely friendship with her father. The man was a bit of an enigma, but he was one of the most successful stock speculators on Wall Street. He'd offered to take Will under his wing as an apprentice of sorts, and Will had been willing to do anything if it meant a stable source of income.

He and Victoria had packed up for America and spent several months in the bustling city of New York. They took a modest home not far from her family's massive Madison Avenue mansion, and Will had thrown himself into learning how to be a financier by day. By night, he came home to his sweet wife. They'd made love in nearly every chamber of that bloody house, and on one of those nights, their son had been conceived.

Alistair William Dalreith, the Viscount of Linton and the future Earl of Pembroke and heir to the Duke of Cranley had been born not long after their return to England. The duke had written with cold congratulations and an edict for the proverbial spare. Will had tossed the letter into the fire where it belonged, savoring the sight of it blackening and curling into ash.

"I'll forever be grateful for that time in New York as

well," he told her with raw honesty. "You and our son are everything to me."

She rolled onto her tiptoes to press a soft kiss to his mouth, sensing what troubled him without him needing to form the ugliness into words. He'd shared the details of his past with her, and she'd been loving and unjudgmental, the light that drove the darkness away. She tasted of tea and sweetness, and he wanted to consume her. He couldn't stop himself from deepening the kiss, angling his lips over hers. He could kiss her a hundred thousand times in his life, and it would still never be enough.

She broke away first, breathless, gazing up at him through lowered lashes. "What will the servants think?"

"That I'm madly in love with my beautiful wife, and that we're ridiculously happy." He grinned. "Or perhaps that New York robbed us of all our manners and we're both of us a hopeless cause. Either way, I don't give a damn."

Her expression turned pensive. "Do you think you'll ever forgive the duke?"

If ever there was a subject that cooled his ardor more than talk of his sire, Will hadn't heard of it yet. "I expect I've already forgiven him, darling. I have to, for the sake of my sanity. But I shan't forget. A man can't choose the family he's born into, but he can damn well choose the family he makes."

The time had come to close the door on the past and its ghosts. Some things were unchangeable. Some deeds could not be undone. But he could build a life with Victoria and Alistair and all the daughters and sons that were yet to come. A whole bushel of them, if he had anything to say about it.

"Oh, Will." She turned into him fully then, her arms twining around his neck. "I'm so happy that you chose me."

He rested their foreheads together, savoring their connectedness, this moment of tranquility and pure bliss. "And I'm so happy you chose me, my love. God knows you shouldn't have after all I'd put you through, but I'll be happy to the end of my days nonetheless."

She licked the seam of his lips, the minx. "Will?"

He was rigid in his trousers. They hadn't made love since little Alistair's birth as her body recovered from the grueling labor, and his body craved hers in the same way that his heart needed her. "Yes, darling?"

"This roof is beautiful, and I'm so pleased that you raised the funds all on your own." She licked him again.

Jesus, she knew how to drive him to distraction. "Yes?"

Victoria gave him a look of feigned innocence. "And Alistair will be napping for the next hour at least, so I really think perhaps we ought to make better use of our time than admiring a roof. It'll be here tomorrow, after all."

He threw back his head and laughed. "A woman of reason. God, I love you."

She pulled away and smiled up at him. "And I love you. Now if you don't mind, I think we are long overdue for a reunion."

He held out his arm for her. "Do you think it will alarm the staff if we take off at a run?"

It was her turn to laugh, the sound joyous and free. "As a wise man so recently said, I don't give a damn."

Read on for an excerpt of Book 2 in the Wicked Husbands Series, *Her Lovestruck Lord*.

Dear Reader,

Thank you for reading *Her Errant Earl!* I hope you enjoyed the first book in the Wicked Husbands series. Fiercely independent, dazzlingly beautiful, and married to handsome scoundrels, these American heiresses are ready to turn the tables on the insufferable English lords they've wed. What happens when their wicked husbands start falling for the wives they never thought they wanted? Corsets come off, bed chambers ignite, the passion sizzles, and more than one stubborn English rake gets reformed by love.

If you'd like to keep up to date with my latest releases, sign up for my email list at:

> http://www.scarsco.com/contact_scarlett.

As always, please consider leaving an honest review of *Her Errant Earl.* All reviews are greatly appreciated!

If you'd like a preview of Book Two in the Wicked Husbands series, do read on.

Until next time,

Scarlett

Her Lovestruck Lord

Wicked Husbands Book Two

She married him for his title…

Maggie, Marchioness of Sandhurst, is trapped in a loveless marriage of convenience. Her husband refused to consummate their union, and she hasn't seen him in over a year. But she has a plan to win back her freedom. All she needs to do is create the scandal of the century.

He married her for her fortune…

Simon, the Marquis of Sandhurst, vowed he'd never touch the wife he didn't want. When he seeks pleasure in the arms of a masked siren at a wicked country house party, he's shocked to discover the woman in question is actually his marchioness.

Will their marriage of convenience become a love match?

As the truth unravels, husband and wife are estranged no longer, spending their days and nights exploring the desire burning hot between them. But when Simon's past comes back to haunt them both, their newfound happiness could be forever dashed.

chapter one

"…love is love for evermore."
-Alfred, Lord Tennyson
England, 1878

MAGGIE, MARCHIONESS OF SANDHURST, knew when to concede defeat, and now was proving just such a moment. She watched the first evening of Lady Needham's infamous country house weekend unfolding in all its raucous glory. How had she ever thought she could find the courage to start a scandal to rival the debauchery before her?

Straight ahead, a masked lady's nipples were nearly visible above the décolletage of her black evening gown as she sipped champagne and flirted shamelessly with a masked gentleman. To her left, a gentleman had a lady pinned to the wall as he feasted on her neck. At her right, another couple's furtive motions suggested they were engaged in something far more depraved.

She'd thought that she was made of stern enough stuff to do what she must to regain her independence. Any man would suffice, she'd told herself, no matter how disagreeable the task. He could be old or young, short or tall, balding, round about the middle. She didn't care. As long as he wasn't cruel or malodorous, she could bear it.

Fool, she chastised herself. *Coward.*

For here she stood, mouth dry, heart thundering in her breast, fingers clenching her silk skirts. Too afraid to step forward, throw caution to the wind. Too fearful to free herself from the prison of her mistakes.

There was no hope for it. She wasn't cut from the same cloth as her fellow revelers, for watching them only made her want to retire to her chamber, snuggle beneath the covers, and read the volume of poetry she'd brought along with her. If only she hadn't chosen duty instead of love.

With a sigh, she turned away from the swirls of skirts and the dashing sight of masked rakes wooing their eager female counterparts. After two steps, she froze as she heard an unmistakable sound above the laughter and the music and the rumble of inebriated voices. It was the one sound a lady never wanted to hear, the sound that invariably made her shudder in her silk shoes.

The awful sound of fabric rending.

Her train, to be specific. The lush fall of silk designed by Worth himself. Hopelessly torn. Dismay mingling with true despair within her, she turned to find the culprit. He was dressed to perfection in evening black, taller than she, his identity obscured by an equally midnight half-mask. The lower half of his face revealed a wide jaw, a sculpted mouth. There was no denying that he was handsome, but he didn't appear to notice her, his glittering green eyes instead traveling the sea of iniquity above Maggie's head.

What a lout. Perhaps he was a drunkard as well. Stifling the urge to roll her eyes in frustration, she attempted to gain the man's attention, for he still stood upon the mangled remnants of her beautiful violet silk. "Pardon me, sir?"

He either ignored her or didn't hear her, caught up in the madness of the ball. For a moment, she had the distinct impression his mind was far away from the ballroom crush.

He seemed to look past them all, lost in his own meandering thoughts.

But this man and his thoughts were not her concern. Be he inebriated, enthralled, or distracted, unfortunately he was still on her skirts. "Sir?" She raised her voice, trying not to call too much attention to herself for she was ashamed she'd even deigned to attend the notorious party in the first place.

He remained oblivious. Perhaps he suffered from a hearing problem. Oh dear. It seemed she had no choice if she wanted to save her train from further damage. Maggie reached out and laid a tentative hand on his arm. "Sir?"

He gave a start and turned the force of that startling mossy gaze on her. "Madam?"

His arm was surprisingly well-muscled, his coat warm with the heat of his large body. She withdrew her touch with haste as if he were a pot too long on the stove that she'd inadvertently touched with her bare hand. He still didn't realize he trampled her gorgeous evening gown. It took her a breath to regain her composure under the force of those piercing eyes.

"Sir," she began hesitantly, "I'm afraid you're standing upon my train. If you'd be so kind?"

"Damn it to hell," he muttered, startling her with his blunt language. His penetrating stare dropped to the floor and he quickly removed the offending shoes from her silk. "Ah Christ, it's ripped to bits, isn't it?"

She cast a dreary eye over the effects of his feet. "I expect it will require some correction, yes."

Correction was rather an understatement. Her silk train, complete with box-pleated ribbon trim and a lace-and-jet overlay, was badly torn. She wasn't certain a seamstress's hand could make repairs without them being obvious to the eye. It wasn't as if she couldn't afford a new gown, but this had been her first occasion wearing it, and it had been unbearably lovely.

"I'm truly sorry." His voice sounded cross, drawing her attention back up to his frowning mouth. "If you'll allow it,

I'll be happy to have it repaired for you."

His mouth was especially fine, she noted again, contrary to her better judgment, firm yet sculpted. He had a generous mouth. Kissable. Dear heaven. What was she about, swooning over an unknown man's lips? Hadn't she just decided she was too craven to create the sort of scandal she'd require? She swallowed, forcing herself to recall what he'd just said.

"I appreciate your offer, sir, but I have a wonderful seamstress." She thought of the dressmaker she used in London when in a pinch. Very likely, the entire train would require replacing.

"But the fault is mine," he persisted, playing the gentleman now that she'd finally gained his attention.

"Nonsense," she parried, feeling slightly foolish over her womanly horror at the damage to her gown. It had not been intentionally done, after all, and she had more than enough coin for Madame Laurier's alterations. "Of all things that need mending, mere fabric is by far the easiest and least costly."

He tilted his head, considering her with a fathomless stare that made her skin tingle to life with a dizzying warmth. "I sincerely doubt truer words were ever spoken."

There was an intensity underlying his words that made her believe he was sincere and not merely another rake plying meaningless flattery. For the first time since stepping into the whirlwind of the ballroom, Maggie was intrigued.

"What have you that needs mending, sir?" she asked, feeling suddenly bold after all.

His lips quirked into a wry smile beneath his mask. "Would you believe it's my heart?"

So he loved another, then. She tried to ignore the stab of disappointment the revelation sent through her. "I know better than anyone just how difficult it is to mend a heart." She frowned as she thought of the unhappy life in which she had found herself. The realization she had settled on this miserable path was a constant burr beneath her mind's saddle. "Perhaps impossible."

"What man would dare to break the heart of a woman as beautiful as you?" he demanded. "An utter imbecile, surely."

She laughed. "Forgive me, but I fear you're guilty of dissembling."

"Dissembling?" He pressed a large hand over his heart, feigning shock. "I'm wounded. Why would you say such a thing?"

"Because you can't see my face," she pointed out, grinning despite herself. She well knew that her dainty mask covered all of her face as well, save her mouth. It was rather the point of a masque, after all. She would have to remove it to accomplish what she wanted. But for now, there was safety in her anonymity.

"Yes, but you have the most extraordinarily lovely eyes I've ever seen," he returned with remarkable aplomb. "I daresay they're almost violet."

Another wave of warmth washed over her. He was somehow different, this man. Dangerous to be sure. "I rather like you," she confided before she could stop herself. Drat. Being too honest had always been one of her downfalls. She'd never been very good at hiding her emotions behind a polite veil. Perhaps it was why she'd had such difficulty blending with London society.

He grinned. "You sound alarmed. I'm not all bad, I assure you."

She shook her head, trying to regain her wits. "It is merely that I'd given up on your countrymen."

"My countrymen?" He paused, his eyes crinkling at the corners as he eyed her with dawning comprehension. "You're an American, are you? I thought I detected an accent."

"I am," she acknowledged. "I suppose that renders my eyes less lovely now." Although a number of American heiresses like herself had made their way to England, they were not always well received. She'd had to work quite hard to forge her way, and acceptance from English ladies had not proved an easy or sometimes even achievable feat.

"Of course not." An emotion she couldn't define darkened his voice. "Your eyes are still lovely as ever. Would you care to dance?"

Oh dear heaven. The invitation excited her until she recalled two things. She was an abysmal dancer, and her train was in pieces. She wisely kept the first to herself. "I'd love to, but I'm afraid my train…"

"Bloody hell, I'd already forgotten." He grimaced. "What an ass. Perhaps you'd like another glass of champagne?"

Belatedly, she realized the glass she held was empty. When had she drunk it all? She couldn't recall. Perhaps that was the reason her head felt as if it had been filled with fluffy white clouds. Yes, that had to be it. Surely it wasn't the tall stranger with the gorgeous mouth who kept plying her with sensual looks and disarming smiles. She probably ought not to have another flute of champagne.

"I'd love another," she said. Hadn't she lived her life the way she should? And what had that gotten her but misery and loneliness and a husband she hadn't seen in over a year?

He returned to her side and pressed another glass of champagne into her hand. "There you are, my dear."

"Thank you." She took a fortifying sip, calming the jagged bundle of her nerves. Perhaps there was hope for her madcap plan after all. The stranger before her would certainly do for a scandal. Yes indeed. He certainly looked like the sort of man who would accept an invitation to sin. She forced her mind into safer territory, trying to distract herself from wanton thoughts. "Who has caused your heart to require mending?" she asked him. "A wife?"

He hesitated, drinking his champagne, and for a moment she feared she'd overstepped her bounds. "Not a wife, no," he said with care. "But a very old and very dear friend."

"A lover," she concluded aloud, then flushed at her bluntness, which always seemed to land her in trouble. "I'm

166

sorry, sir, if I'm too forthright. I cannot seem to help myself."

"You needn't apologize. Everyone knows that here at Lady Needham's none of the standard society rules apply. You've but to look around you to see that." His tone was wry as his gaze lit on the couple against the wall. The man had caught the woman's skirts in his fist, raising them to reveal her shapely, stocking-clad calves.

Maggie looked away, cheeks stinging. Of course none of the standard rules applied here. Indeed, from all appearances, there were *no* rules here. It was one of the many reasons she'd decided—against her better judgment—to attend. What better place to create a scandal than a party that existed for the express purpose of licentiousness?

"Is that why you're here?" she asked him, unable to squelch her curiosity. "For the…lack of rules?"

Surely it was the champagne that made her so daring. For the real Maggie would never have dreamt of insinuating such a thing to a stranger. She'd all but asked him if he sought a lover, for heaven's sake. But if she wanted to succeed in forcing her husband to divorce her, she couldn't be herself. She had to be someone fearless and bold. Someone without conscience.

"I suppose it is in part," he confirmed, taking another sip of spirits. "What of you? What brings you here? You appear terribly young for this fast set."

"Disappointment, I suppose." She gulped her champagne as he closed the distance between them. He was so near she could see the dark stubble on his defined jaw.

"You're certainly too young for disappointment." He ran a finger from her elbow to her wrist, stopping to tangle his fingers with hers. "Who would dare to disappoint you?"

"My husband," she whispered, her mouth going dry. Though truth be told, she was far more disappointed in herself than she was in the marquis. After all, she had known he married her for her dowry in the same way she had married him for his title. It was simply that she had not anticipated his utter defection and her resulting misery. But there was little need to divulge her inner sins and secrets to the man before her now. This was to be a lighthearted affair. A means to an end.

"He must be an utter bastard to cause you so much distress."

She laughed without mirth. "I would simply say he is a rather cold and heartless man." Yes indeed, that described Sandhurst perfectly.

He squeezed her fingers. "I'm sorry, my dear."

"You are not the man who owes me an apology." The old sadness bloomed in her heart as she thought of Jonathan and all she'd left behind. "But I suppose I'll never have one from him." The best she could expect from him was anger. Perhaps a blinding fury. She meant to cuckold him before all of London, to leave no doubt in the minds of the entire *ton*. Only then could she be free. This man could help her. She felt certain of it.

"Do you love him?" he asked, startling her.

His query threw her. People of their class so rarely married for love. She did not love her husband, but she had certainly married him with a hopeful heart. Her mother had assured her that many modern marriages began with respect and led to tender affections after time and diligence. She had hoped to foster a relationship of kindness between herself and her husband, at the very least. Instead, their relationship simply consisted of silence. But it was odd for the man before her to have even pondered such a question.

"Of course not," she said at last. "What of you and your very dear friend? Do you love her?"

"I did for many years," he said, the admission seemingly torn from him. "Now, I'm not certain what I feel any longer. A need for change, certainly."

She saw them for what they were then, a man and woman who had somehow run across each other's paths at the same ball, both of them lost. Searching. She longed to escape from the gilded prison in which she now found herself. He longed for something. Perhaps distraction. A lover. It didn't matter. What did matter was that the fear in her had at long last subsided. She stood ready, poised to grab the reins of her life and steer herself in a different direction.

"What sort of change do you seek?" she asked, watching him above the rim of her flute.

His sinful mouth curved in a half smile. "I think perhaps it's you."

She nearly choked on her mouthful of champagne. "Me?"

"Oh yes," he told her in that seductive, deep voice of his. His green eyes were fierce and direct on her, trapping her gaze so she couldn't look anywhere else. There was no denying his sensual promise. "You."

Her Lovestruck Lord is available now. Get your copy today.

If you enjoy steamy Regency and Victorian romance, don't miss the Heart's Temptation series. Read on for an excerpt of Book One, *A Mad Passion*.

A lost love…

Seven years ago, the Marquis of Thornton broke Cleo's heart, and she hasn't forgotten or forgiven him. But when she finds him standing before her at a country house party, as devastatingly handsome as ever, old temptations prove difficult to resist. One stolen kiss is all it takes.

A proper gentleman…

Thornton buried his past and his feelings for Cleo long ago. He's worked diligently to become a respected politician with a reputation above reproach. The only trouble in his otherwise perfect life is that he can't resist the maddening beauty he never stopped wanting, no matter how devastating the cost.

A mad passion…

Cleo is hopelessly trapped in a loveless marriage, and Thornton is on the cusp of making an advantageous match to further his political ambitions. The more time they spend in each other's arms, the more they court scandal and ruin. Theirs is a love that was never meant to be. Or is it?

chapter one

*"A beautiful woman risking
everything for a mad passion."*
– *Oscar Wilde*

Wilton House, September 1880

CLEO, COUNTESS SCARBROUGH, decided there had never been a more ideal moment to feign illness. The very last thing she wanted to do was traipse through wet grass at a country house party while her dress improver threatened to crush her. Not to mention the disagreeable prospect of being forced to endure the man before her. What had her hostess been thinking to pair them together? Did she not know of their history? A treasure hunt indeed.

Seven years and the Marquis of Thornton hadn't changed a whit, damn him. Tall and commanding, he was arrogance personified standing amidst the other glittering lords and ladies. Oh, perhaps his shoulders had broadened and she noted fine lines 'round his intelligent gray eyes. But not even a kiss of silver strands earned from his demanding

171

career in politics marred the glorious black hair. It was most disappointing. After all, there had been whispers following the Prime Minister's successful Midlothian Campaign that a worn-out Thornton would retire from politics and his unofficial position as Gladstone's personal aid altogether. But as far as she could discern, the man staring down upon her was the same insufferably handsome man who had betrayed her. Was it so much to ask that he'd at least become plump about the middle?

Truly. A treasure hunt? Gads and to think this was the most anticipated house party of the year. "I'm afraid I must retire to my chamber," she announced to him. "I have a megrim."

Just as she began to breathe easier, Thornton ruined her reprieve. His sullen mouth quirked into a disengaged smile. "I'll escort you."

"You needn't trouble yourself." She hadn't meant for him to play the role of gentleman. She just wanted to be rid of him.

Thornton's face was an impenetrable mask. "It's no trouble."

"Indeed." Dismay sank through her like a stone. There was no way to extricate herself without being quite obvious he still set her at sixes and sevens. "Lead the way."

He offered his arm and she took it, aware that in her eagerness to escape him, she had just entrapped herself more fully. Instead of staying in the safe, boring company of the other revelers, she was leaving them at her back. Perhaps a treasure hunt would not have been so terrible a fate.

An uncomfortable silence fell between them, with Cleo aware the young man who had dizzied her with stolen kisses had aged into a cool, imperturbable stranger. For all the passion he showed now, she could have been a buttered parsnip on his plate.

She told herself she didn't give a straw for him, that walking a short distance just this once would have no effect on her. Even if he did smell somehow delectable and not at all as some gentlemen did of tobacco and horse. No. His was a masculine, alluring scent of sandalwood and spice. And his arm beneath her hand felt as strongly corded with muscle as it looked under his coat.

"You have changed little, Lady Scarbrough," Thornton offered at last when they were well away from the others, en route to Wilton House's imposing façade. "Lovely as ever."

"You are remarkably civil, my lord," she returned, not patient enough for a meaningless, pleasant exchange. She didn't wish to cry friends with him. There was too much between them.

His jaw stiffened and she knew she'd finally irked him. "Did you think to find me otherwise?"

"Our last parting was an ugly one." Perverse, perhaps, but she wanted to remind him, couldn't bridle her tongue. She longed to grab handfuls of his fine coat and shake him. What right did he have to appear so smug, so handsome? To be so self-assured, refined, magnetic?

"I had forgotten." Thornton's tone, like the sky above them, remained light, nonchalant.

"Forgotten?" The nerve of the man! He had acted the part of lovelorn suitor well enough back then.

"It was, what, all of ten years past, no?"

"Seven," she corrected before she could think better of it.

He smiled down at her as if he were a kindly uncle regarding a pitiable orphaned niece. "Remarkable memory, Lady Scarbrough."

"One would think your memory too would recall such an occasion, even given your advanced age."

"How so?" He sounded bored, deliberately overlooking her jibe at his age which was, if she were honest, only thirty to her five and twenty. "We never would have suited." His gray eyes melted into hers, his grim mouth tipping upward in what would have been a grin on any other man. Thornton didn't grin. He smoldered.

Drat her stays. Too tight, too tight. She couldn't catch a breath. Did he mean to be cruel? Cleo knew a great deal about not suiting. She and Scarbrough had been at it nearly since the first night they'd spent as man and wife. He had crushed her, hurt her, grunted over her and gone to his mistress.

"Of course we wouldn't suit," she agreed. Still, inwardly she had to admit there had been many nights in her early marriage where she had lain awake, listening for Scarbrough's footfalls, wondering if she hadn't chosen a Sisyphean fate.

They entered Wilton House and began the lengthy tromp to its Tudor revival styled wing where many of the guests had been situated. Thornton placed a warm hand over hers. He gazed down at her with a solemn expression, some of the arrogance gone from his features. "I had not realized you would be in attendance, Lady Scarbrough."

"Nor I you." She was uncertain of what, if any, portent hid in his words. Was he suggesting he was not as immune as he pretended? She wished he had not insisted upon escorting her.

As they drew near the main hall, a great commotion arose. Previously invisible servants sprang forth, bustling with activity. A new guest had arrived and Cleo recognized the strident voice calling out orders. Thornton's hand stiffened over hers and his strides increased. She swore she overheard him mumble something like 'not yet, damn it', but couldn't be sure. To test him, she stopped. Her heavy skirts swished front then back, pulling her so she swayed into him.

Cleo cast him a sidelong glance. "My lord, I do believe your mother is about to grace us with her rarified presence."

He growled, losing some of his polish like a candlestick too long overlooked by the rag. "Nonsense. We mustn't tarry. You've the headache." He punctuated his words with a sharp, insolent yank on her arm to get her moving.

She beamed. "I find it begins to dissipate."

The dowager Marchioness of Thornton had a certain reputation. She was a lioness with an iron spine, an undeterred sense of her own importance and enough consequence to cut anyone she liked. Cleo knew the dowager despised her. She wouldn't dare linger to incur her wrath were it not so painfully obvious the good woman's own son was desperate to avoid her. And deuce it, she wanted to see Thornton squirm.

"Truly, I would not importune you by forcing you to wait in the hall amidst the chill air," he said, quite stuffy now, no longer bothering to tug her but pulling her down the hall as if he were a mule and she his plow.

The shrill voice of her ladyship could be heard admonishing the staff for their posture. Thornton's pace increased, directing them into the wrong wing. She was about to protest when the dowager called after him. It seemed the saint still feared his mother.

"Goddamn." Without a moment of hesitation, he opened the nearest door, stepped inside and pulled her through with him.

Cleo let out a disgruntled 'oof' as she sank into the confines of whatever chamber Thornton had chosen as their hiding place. The door clicked closed and darkness descended in the cramped quarters.

"Thornton," trilled the marchioness, her voice growing closer.

"Your—" Cleo began speaking, but Thornton's hand over her mouth muffled the remainder of her words. She inhaled, startled by the solid presence of his large body so close behind her. Her bustle crushed against him.

"Hush, please. I haven't the patience for my mother today."

He meant to avoid the dragon for the entire day? Did he really think it possible? She shifted, discomfited by his nearness. Goodness, the little room was stifling. Her stays pinched her again. Did he need to smell so divine?

"Argnnnthhwt," she replied.

175

She needed air. The cramped quarters dizzied her. Certainly it wasn't the proximity of her person to Thornton that played mayhem with her senses. Absolutely not. The ridiculous man simply had to take his hand from her mouth. Why, he was nearly cutting off her air. She could scarcely breathe.

Thornton didn't seem likely to oblige her, so she resorted to tactics learned from growing up with a handful of sisters who were each more than a handful themselves. She decided not to play fair and licked his palm. It was a mistake, a terrible one and not just because it was unladylike but because he tasted salty and sweet. He tasted rather like something she might want to nibble. So she did the unpardonable. She licked him again.

"Christ." To her mingled relief and disappointment, he removed his hand. "Say a word and I'll throttle you."

Footsteps sounded in the hall just beyond the closed door. If Cleo had been tempted to end their ruse before, her sudden reaction to Thornton rattled her too much to do so now. She kept mum.

"Perhaps you are mistaken?" Thornton's sister, Lady Bella ventured, sounding meek.

"Don't be an idiot, Bella," the dowager snapped. "I know my own son when I see him. All your novels are making you addle-pated. How many times must I implore you to assert yourself at more improving endeavors like needlepoint? Women should not be burdened by knowledge. Our constitutions are too delicate."

Cleo couldn't quite stifle a snicker. The situation had all the elements of a comedy. All that yet remained was for the dowager to yank open the door so Cleo and Thornton would come tumbling out.

"You smell of lavender," he muttered in her ear, an accusation.

So what if she did? It was a lovely, heady scent blended specifically for her. Lavender and rose geranium, to be precise. "Hold your breath," she retorted, "if you find it so objectionable."

"I don't."

"Then what is the problem, Thornton?"

"I find it delicious."

Delicious. It was a word of possibility, of improbability, improper and yet somehow…seductive. Enticing. Yes, dear heaven, the man enticed her. She leaned into his solid presence, her neck seeking. Even better, her neck's sensitive skin found his hungry mouth.

He tasted her, licking her skin, nipping in gentle bites, trying, it would seem, to consume her like a fine dessert. His hands anchored her waist. Thornton pulled her back against him, all semblance of hauteur gone. Her dress improver cut viciously into her sides.

She didn't care. She forgot about his mother. Their quarrel and complicated past flitted from her mind. Cleo reached behind her with her right arm and sank her fingers into his hair. He stilled, then tore his lips from her neck. Neither of them moved. Their breaths blended. Thornton's hands splayed over her bodice, possessive and firm.

"This is very likely a mistake," he murmured.

"Very likely so," she agreed and then pressed her mouth to his.

He kissed her as she hadn't been kissed in years. Strike that. He kissed her as she hadn't been kissed in her lifetime, deep and hard and consuming. He kissed her like he wanted to claim her, mark her. And she kissed him back with all the passion she hadn't realized she possessed. Dear heavens, this was not the political saint who took her mouth with such force but the sinner she'd once known. Had she thought him cold?

Thornton twisted her until her back slammed against the door with a thud. His tongue swept into her mouth. Her hands gripped his strong shoulders, pulling him closer. An answering ache blossomed within her. Somehow, he found his way under her skirts, grasping her left leg at the knee and hooking it around his lean hip. Deliberate fingers trailed up her thigh beneath three layers of fabric, finding bare skin. He skimmed over lacy drawers, dipping inside to tease her.

When he sank two fingers inside her, she gasped, yanking back into the door again. It rattled. Voices murmured from far away in the hall. "Thornton," she whispered. "We should stop."

He dropped a hot kiss on her neck, then another. "Absolutely. This is folly."

Then he belied his words by shifting her so her body pressed against his instead of the door. She no longer cared why they should stop. Her good intentions dissipated. Her bodice suddenly seemed less snug and she realized he had undone a few buttons. Heavens. The icy man of moments ago bore no resemblance to the man setting her body aflame. Scarbrough had never touched her this way, had never made her feel giddy and tingly, as if she might fly up into the clouds.

Scarbrough. Just the thought of her husband stiffened her spine. Hadn't she always sworn to herself she would not be like him? Here she was, nearly making love in who knew what manner of chamber with Thornton, a man she didn't even find pleasant. The man, to be specific, who had betrayed and abandoned her. How could she be so wanton and foolish to forget what he'd done for a few moments of pleasure?

She pushed him away, breathing heavy, heart heavy. "We must stop."

"Why must we?" He caressed her arms, wanting to seduce her again.

"My husband."

"I don't hear him outside the door."

"Nor do I, but I am not a society wife even if my conduct with you suggests otherwise. I do not make love with men in closets at country house parties. I don't fall to his level."

"Madam, your husband is a louse. You could not fall to his level were you to roll in the hay with every groom in our hostess' stable and then run naked through the drawing room."

She stiffened. "What do you know of him?"

"Plenty."

"I doubt you do." The inescapable urge to defend her wastrel, blackguard husband rose within her. How dare Thornton be so arrogant, so condescending when he himself had committed the same sins against her? And had he not just been on the verge of making love to a married woman in a darkened room? He was no better.

He sighed. "Scarbrough's got scads of women on the wrong side of the Park in St. John's Wood. It's common knowledge."

Of course it was, but that didn't make it any easier to hear. Especially not coming from Thornton, the man she'd jilted in favor of Scarbrough. "I'm aware Scarbrough is indiscreet, but that has little bearing on you and me in this moment. This moment should never have happened."

"We are once again in agreement, Cleo." His voice regained some of its arrogance. "However, it did happen."

Her name on his lips startled her, but she didn't bother taking him to task for it. After the intimacies she had just allowed, it would be hypocritical. She wished she could see him. The darkness became unbearable.

"How could you so easily forget your own sins? You had your pretty little actress all the while you claimed to love me."

He said nothing. Silence extended between them. It was obstinate of her, but she wanted him to deny it. Thornton did not.

"Aren't there orphans about somewhere you should be saving?" She lashed out, then regretted her angry words. That was badly done of her. But this, being in Thornton's arms after what he'd done...it went against the grain.

"I think you should go," she added.

"I would if I could fight my way past your bloody skirts. There's no help for it. Either you go first or we go together."

"We can't go together! Your insufferable mother may be

lurking out there somewhere."

"Then you must go first."

"I shall precede you," she informed him.

"I already suggested as much. Twice, if you had but listened." He sounded peeved.

The urge to stamp her foot hit her with fierce persistence. "You are a vexing man."

"And you, my love, are a shrew unless your mouth is otherwise occupied."

She gasped. "How dare you?"

"Oh, I dare lots of things. Some of them, you may even like." His voice had gone sinful and dark.

The dreadful man. She drew herself up in full countess armor. "I'm leaving now."

Then he ruined her consequence by saying, "Lovely. Though you might want to fasten up your bodice before you go. I should think it terribly difficult to convince my mother we were talking about the weather when your finer bits are on display."

Her finer bits? It was the outside of enough. She slapped his arm. "Has the Prime Minister any idea what a coarse scoundrel you are? None of my…person would be on display if you hadn't pulled me into the room and accosted me."

"You were well pleased for a woman being accosted," he pointed out, smug.

She hated him again, which was really for the best. He was too much of a temptation, too delicious, to borrow his word, and she was ever a fool for him. "You're insufferable."

"So I've been told."

Cleo gave him her back and attempted to fasten her buttons. Drat. She pulled. She held her breath. She tugged her bodice's stiff fabric again. The buttons wouldn't meet their moorings. "Did you undo my lacings?" she demanded, realization dawning on her.

"Perhaps." Thornton's voice had gone wistful. Sheepish,

almost.

Good heavens. How did he know his way around a woman's undergarments so well he could get her undone and partially unlaced all while kissing her passionately? Beneath his haughty exterior still lay a womanizer's heart.

There was no help for it now. She couldn't tight-lace herself. "I require some assistance," she mumbled.

"What was that?"

Cleo gritted her teeth. "I can't lace myself."

"Would a 'please' be in order?"

"You're the one who did the damage. It seems reasonable that you should repair it."

"Perhaps I can slip past your voluminous skirts after all," he mused.

"Please help me," she blurted.

"Turn around," he ordered.

Cleo spun, reluctant to face him again. She could barely see him in the murkiness, a tall, imposing figure. His hands slipped inside her bodice, expertly finding the lacings he had loosened.

"Breathe in," he told her.

She did and he pulled tightly, cinching her waist to a painful wasp silhouette once more. "Thank you. I can manage the buttons."

He spun her about and brushed aside her fingers. "I'll get them." She swore she heard a smile in his voice. "After all, it only seems reasonable I repair the damage I've done."

"Fine then." His breath fanned her lips and she could feel his intense gaze on her. She tilted her head to the side to ease her disquiet at his nearness. Was it just her imagination, or did his fingers linger at the buttons nearest her bosom?

"There you are." Thornton fastened the last one, brushing the hollow of her throat as he did so.

She closed her eyes and willed away the desire that assaulted her. This man was not for her. He ran the backs of his fingers along her neck, stopping when he cupped her jaw.

"Thank you," she whispered again.

"You're most welcome," he said, voice low.

The magnetism between them was inexorable, just as it had been before. Despite the intervening years, despite all, she still recalled the way he had made her feel—weightless and enchanted, as though she had happened upon Shakespeare's moonlit forest in *A Midsummer Night's Dream*.

His thumb brushed over her bottom lip. "If you don't go, I'll undo all the repairing I've just done."

She knew he warned himself as much as he warned her. Sadness pulsed between them, a mutual acknowledgment their lives could have turned up differently. So many unspoken words, so much confusion lingered.

"I must go," she said unnecessarily. She was reluctant to leave him and that was the plain truth of it. "I find my megrim has returned."

With that, she left, returning to the hall, to sunlight streaming in cathedral windows. More importantly, she hoped, she returned to sanity.

A Mad Passion is available now. Get your copy today.

Don't miss Scarlett's other romances!
(Listed by Series)

HISTORICAL ROMANCE

Heart's Temptation

A Mad Passion (Book One)
Rebel Love (Book Two)
Reckless Need (Book Three)
Sweet Scandal (Book Four)
Restless Rake (Book Five Coming Soon)

Wicked Husbands

Her Errant Earl (Book One)
Her Lovestruck Lord (Book Two)
Her Reformed Rake (Book Three Coming Soon)

CONTEMPORARY ROMANCE

Love's Second Chance

Reprieve (Book One)
Perfect Persuasion (Book Two)
Win My Love (Book Three)

Coastal Heat

Loved Up (Book One)

about the author

Award-winning author Scarlett Scott writes contemporary and historical romance with heat, heart, and happily ever afters. Since publishing her first book in 2010, she has become a wife, mother to adorable identical twins and one TV-loving dog, and a killer karaoke singer. Well, maybe not the last part, but that's what she'd like to think.

A self-professed literary junkie and nerd, she loves reading anything but especially romance novels, poetry, and Middle English verse. When she's not reading, writing, wrangling toddlers, or camping, you can catch up with her on her website www.scarsco.com. Hearing from readers never fails to make her day.

Scarlett's complete book list and information about upcoming releases can be found on her website.

Follow Scarlett on social media:

www.instagram.com/scarlettscottauthor
www.twitter.com/scarscoromance
www.pinterest.com/scarlettscott
www.facebook.com/AuthorScarlettScott

10028661R00113

Printed in Germany
by Amazon Distribution
GmbH, Leipzig